D0845160

The Veil of Ignorance

Sister Mary Teresa mysteries by Monica Quill:

The Veil of Ignorance
Sine Qua Nun
Nun of the Above
And Then There Was Nun
Let Us Prey
Not a Blessed Thing

The Veil of Ignorance

A Sister Mary Teresa Mystery

by
Monica Quill

St.
Martin's
Press
•
*New
York*

DESIGN BY DEBBY JAY

Library of Congress Cataloging-in-Publication Data

McInerny, Ralph M.
        The veil of ignorance / Monica Quill.
                p. cm.
        ISBN 0-312-02308-1
        I. Title.
    PS3563.A31166V45 1988
    813'.54—dc 19   88-16886
                                                           CIP

First Edition

10 9 8 7 6 5 4 3 2 1

The Veil of Ignorance

One

T wenty-four hours after her release from prison, Lydia Hopkins appeared at the house on Walton Street and asked to see Sister Mary Teresa Dempsey.

Kim's instinctive reaction was to block the doorway, and her urge to close the door on the all-too-familiar face was strong.

"This is where she lives, isn't it?"

The decision of Judge Marsha Hunter to grant Lydia her freedom had been greeted with almost universal condemnation, and for several days prior to Lydia's release from prison the events that had led to her conviction were sensational fare on daily television and in the Chicago press. Sister Mary Teresa had made impatient noises and shaken her head in disapproval. And not of the judge.

"How vindictive people are. Well, not people perhaps. Journalists. Listen to them snarl."

If Emtee Dempsey thus instinctively took the part of the

underdog, Kim was less willing to see in Lydia Hopkins a wronged woman. The photographs of her murdered husband and child were all the more poignant for being snapshots found in the family album. The balding man with a light beard, the beautiful child smiling into the few months remaining to her on this earth. On television grim-faced men carried rubberized body bags down the driveway of the Hopkins home in Elmhurst again and again, the event immortalized by a camera crew and now, nearly three years later, resurrected for the titillation of television viewers.

"I wonder when she'll come see me," Emtee Dempsey had murmured.

"Why on earth would she do that?"

Clear blue eyes looked pensively at Kim but the old nun said nothing more. Kim dismissed it as pardonable megalomania. Emtee Dempsey, thanks to a series of accidental involvements and lucky guesses—this is how Kim's brother, Richard, would have put it—had come to think of herself as self-appointed ombudsman for those suspected of crime, at least if they also happened to be former students of hers, alumnae of the college west of the city once conducted by the Order of Martha and Mary before its precipitous decline in the wake of Vatican II. The once-flourishing order now consisted of three nuns in this house on Walton Street where Emtee Dempsey was completing her massive history of the twelfth century. Kim was a graduate student at Northwestern and research assistant to the old nun, and Joyce took care of the house.

"Did Lydia Hopkins attend our college?" Kim asked.

"Not that I know of. I doubt that she would have been old enough while the place was still open."

"Then why do you think she'll come here?" Kim felt she had fallen into a trap or, worse, was feeding Emtee Dempsey's fancy that she was a standing corrective to the

2

flaws of the legal system in general and that of the city of Chicago in particular.

"We have been in correspondence for some time."

Incredible as that seemed, it was possible. Besides, Emtee Dempsey would never lie. She was a past mistress of the mental reservation, all too adroit in permitting people to believe the opposite of the truth, but such a simple declarative sentence wore its meaning on its face, and Kim had no choice but to accept it as true. What she need not and did not accept was the supposition that the infamous murderess of Elmhurst would hurry to Emtee Dempsey as soon as she had achieved her tainted freedom.

Three years after her conviction and trial and several unsuccessful appeals, Lydia Hopkins had been released because Judge Marsha Hunter, speaking *in propria persona* because the State Supreme Court was not in session, declared there had been serious defects in her trial. On a legal technicality, a woman found guilty of murdering her husband and child was granted her freedom. No wonder the media were furious. JUDGE HUNTER DOES IT AGAIN cried a headline in the *Elmhurst Aurora Dawn*.

Joyce got from the public library a battered copy of *Suburban Bloodbath*, the sensational account of the Hopkins murders written by two city reporters. In the book, the hearsay and guesses and speculation that could not be introduced in court made the case against Lydia more damning still. Not that the evidence presented in court had left any doubt of her guilt.

Now, face to face with Lydia Hopkins in the doorway of the house on Walton Street, Kim had little choice but to invite her in.

"She's expecting you," she managed to say.

The impassive face did not change expression, though a movement of the eyes suggested the remark pleased her. Had she schooled herself against emotion and feeling? If

3

hope is never admitted to the heart, disappointment can be held at bay.

Lydia followed Kim down the hall to the old nun's study. Emtee Dempsey turned slowly in her chair when Kim announced that Lydia Hopkins had come to see her. The old nun rose to her feet and came without the aid of her cane to the doorway. Only a few seconds' hesitation, and then she took the murderess in her arms.

Kim was not invited to stay. The almost invariable rule was that she be present whenever visitors called. To be dismissed was unusual and, in this case, maddening. Kim would have given much to hear what the released prisoner and the old nun would say to one another. She entered the kitchen in an angry mood, making unnecessary noise getting a mug from the cupboard.

"I just put on a fresh pot," Joyce said, frowning over her crossword puzzle. "It'll be ready in a minute. Who was at the door?"

"Lydia Hopkins."

"Ha."

"I wasn't asked to stay."

Joyce did not look up. "Who was it really?"

"Lydia Hopkins, as predicted. Emtee hugged her like a lost relative."

Kim had not told Joyce of the correspondence Sister Mary Teresa claimed to have with Lydia Hopkins. The more she had thought about it, the more likely it seemed that the old nun's seemingly simple statement could bear an interpretation other than that she had been literally corresponding with Lydia Hopkins. Kim had been burned too often by underestimating the old nun's subtlety. As had her brother, Detective Lieutenant Richard Moriarity of the Chicago police.

"I was taught to call it lying," he said. "Of course that was by a different kind of nun."

4

"Sister Mary Teresa never lies."

"In those days nuns looked like nuns, of course." Richard lifted his eyes as if searching for a better past. It was small of him, turning on her when his gripe was with Emtee Dempsey. The old nun still wore the traditional habit of the order founded by Blessed Abigail Keineswegs in Bavaria, but Kim and Joyce did not.

"You don't wear a uniform," Kim replied.

"I'm a plainclothes detective."

"I'm a plainclothes nun."

"You can say that again."

How infuriating he could be. Did he treat his wife like this? The thought made her own life seem less of a sacrifice. Imagine being tied to someone like Richard!

Joyce looked doubly betrayed, by Emtee Dempsey and by Kim as well. That she had been kept in the dark about the chance that Lydia Hopkins might show up at their door was worse than unfair. Joyce thrived on such bonuses as this of living with Emtee Dempsey. So do I, Kim told herself. Why else was she so peeved at not being asked to remain in the study?

Two and a half cups of dawdled-over coffee later, the door of the study opened. Footsteps came down the hall, the distinctive shuffle of the old nun, the almost silent tread of Lydia Hopkins. Kim did not move. Let Emtee Dempsey show her guest out.

But Emtee Dempsey brought Lydia into the kitchen.

"Is there coffee made?" she asked with uncharacteristic heartiness. Kim wondered if her expression when she opened the door had been as revealing as Joyce's now. Opening the cupboard, Kim took down a mug.

"Do you want a cup, Sister?"

The old nun shook her head. "Sister Joyce, would you help Lydia get settled in the apartment downstairs? She'll be staying with us. Sister Kimberly, come with me."

5

Kim followed the old nun back to the study and closed the door after them. Emtee Dempsey got settled at her desk, picked up her fountain pen, held it in both hands, and thought for a moment.

"I will need that awful book on Anselm of Canterbury after all, Sister. I thought I would ignore it, but I've decided I can't."

"How long will she stay?"

Emtee Dempsey pretended not to understand. Then feigned comprehension illumined her face.

"Lydia? I really don't know. Maybe for a very long time."

"Can you guess? Joyce will want to know."

The corners of the pursed little mouth twitched and then came a bright smile.

"Sister, she wants to stay! She thinks she has a vocation. Lydia Hopkins wants to be a nun."

Kim and Joyce might be surprised by Emtee Dempsey's decision to offer sanctuary to Lydia Hopkins, they might be happy or unhappy with it, but finally they had no say in the matter. The old nun was their religious superior and had no inclination whatsoever to water the discipline of the Order of Martha and Mary with democracy, even though the house on Walton Street was only a remnant of an order. Nor was she moved by the thought that the order's mode of governance had not saved it from tumult and defection.

"That was to annoy you," Joyce said when Kim repeated Emtee Dempsey's enigmatic remark about Lydia Hopkins's vocation.

Perhaps she was right. It is not necessary to be a saint in order to become a nun, but being a public sinner is an equivocal recommendation. Of course, even to think such thoughts was to hear responses to them. Jesus shamed those who condemned the woman taken in adultery. Kim certainly did not want to voice her doubts to Emtee Dempsey. The old nun would have been capable of depicting her own prereligious life over a half century ago as one of riot and abandon, the better to make Lydia seem the most ordinary of aspirants. Anyway, Joyce could be right that Emtee Dempsey was only teasing.

Lydia was settled in the basement apartment and for the first several days Joyce brought her meals down to her. It was as though they were all in a transition period, getting used to one another. Joyce referred to Lydia as "the postulant," which didn't help. Kim took the opportunity to get as clear as she could on the murders of Jeffrey and little Laura Hopkins (the newspapers had invariably referred to Lydia's daughter as "Little Laura") to see if Emtee Dempsey's decision to champion the convicted murderess was due to something other than her customary perversity.

The body of Jeffrey Hopkins had been found one gray February day in the basement of the family home in Elmhurst. A 911 call was placed at two in the afternoon and the recording of it had been played at the trial, on television, on radio. The tiny frightened voice on the line was held to be that of little Laura, perhaps the last words she had ever spoken. The call was abruptly cut off. For half an hour the operators of the Elmhurst 911 system discussed the call. They were inclined to think it a hoax. They actually voted on whether or not to sound the alarm. By the time the first patrol car pulled into the Hopkins driveway, little Laura, like her father, was dead.

The child was found just inside the front door, which, despite the weather, stood open. A trail of blood from the child's body led to a closed door in the basement. Jeffrey Hopkins had been a handyman; his workshop was a putterer's delight. He could not have imagined when he bought it that the lightweight battery-driven band saw would be the instrument of his own death. If indeed it had been. One of the more grisly moments of the trial was devoted to determining whether Jeffrey Hopkins had already been dead when his murderer went to work on him with the saw. After all, he had been shot four times with a .22 pistol. A whole clip had been emptied to get those four shots into him. The police dug slugs out of the walls and woodwork of the first floor, as well as the basement, and that fact played a major role in Prosecutor Manuel Carrillo's reconstruction of the events of that February day.

Establishing that the Hopkins marriage had been an unhappy one was easy enough. Relatives, neighbors, business associates of Jeffrey's all agreed. One or both of the Hopkinses had picked a lemon in the garden of love and it seemed only a matter of time before they broke up. Two days before the murders, there had been a public scene between the Hopkinses at Elm Stand Country Club. Upon discovering Lydia having lunch with Bill Dunning, a lawyer, Jeffrey objected loudly, and an infuriated Lydia had loudly reported on Jeffrey's transgressions. As he left the room, she narrowly missed him with a heavy glass ashtray she hurled. The waiter overheard her say to Dunning that she would kill that sonofabitch yet. Dunning's memory failed him and he was unsure if that was precisely what Lydia had said. That she had been angry was obvious to anyone, but the lawyer could recall no specific threat. The following day, Lydia rammed her car repeatedly into her husband's. His had been parked in the driveway when the garage door opened. Lydia backed into the street, threw her car in gear, and took a run at the back of Jeffrey's car. The second crash brought him running from the house. He tried to get into his own car, perhaps to get it out of harm's way, but Lydia redoubled her efforts and managed to jam the car into the open garage. Lydia backed into the street and drove off. Half an hour later a wrecker came,

8

extricated Jeffrey's car from the garage, and hauled it away. Subsequently, father and daughter had gone off in a cab.

On the day of the murder, the neighbors had noticed nothing before Lydia dashed from the front door, leaving it ajar, ran to her car parked in the street, and drove off at a reckless speed. No shots had been heard. The neighbors, chiefly Mrs. Hughes, who lived directly across the street from the Hopkinses, had thought little of this swift departure until the police pulled into the driveway and the incredible killings came to light. Mrs. Hughes had unhesitatingly answered the series of questions put her by Manuel Carrillo that placed Lydia's departure between the 911 call and the arrival of the police.

The .22 pistol was found in a St. Vincent de Paul Society bin in the parking lot of the supermarket Lydia frequented. The pistol had been flung in among used clothes destined for the unfortunate. It had been wiped clean of fingerprints—except for several slightly smudged ones of Jeffrey Hopkins. No prints were found on the handle of the saw. The instrument that had been used to kill little Laura had never been found; the conjecture was that it had been a golf club and Lydia's clubs were missing from her locker at the country club, to which she had fled from the Hopkins house. The lab crew ran tests on the inside of Lydia's locker. The few drops of blood they discovered proved to be Laura's, and several strands of her blond hair were also found in the locker.

Manuel Carrillo assured the jury they would never find a case clearer than this. There was motive. There had been a threat. There was physical evidence. There was the testimony of witnesses. The men and women of the jury, he suggested, were vicarious eyewitnesses to the deed itself. They could see Lydia pursuing her husband through the house, shooting wildly. She had followed him to his workroom where he had taken refuge and shot him again and

9

again. Then, her rage still unsatisfied, she savagely mutilated his body with an electric saw. Nor was her rage yet
spent. When she discovered her daughter on the phone,
she had cut the connection, dragged the child to the grisly
scene below, perhaps forcing little Laura to see her bloody
handiwork, then unnaturally turned on the fruit of her
own womb with a golf club and beat her to death. Having
done these dreadful things, she was mad enough to think
she could divert the hand of justice. She had cleaned the
handle of the saw. She took the pistol with her when she
fled the house and tossed it into the St. Vincent De Paul
used-clothes bin. At the club, she first put the iron with
which she had bludgeoned her daughter into her locker,
but then thought better of it and got rid of the bag and all
its contents. Who knew what lake or river that golf bag
now lay at the bottom of?

What did Lydia have to offer in her own defense? Her
story of fleeing the house because her husband was threatening her with the .22 pistol had brought looks of incredulity to the jurors' faces. And where had she fled? First
to the country club, where she had calmed herself by en-
gaging the former pro, Adam Fenwick, in conversation,
then to the office of William Dunning. She'd reached the
end of her rope; she wanted to talk divorce. Carrillo had
managed to get Dunning on the stand, but there was no
way in the world the defense lawyer was going to be forced
to reveal such privileged information. Reporters had de-
tected relief in the lawyer's manner. Only a massive failure
of memory could have enabled him to avoid giving testimony that would have made an airtight case tighter still.

The jury delivered its verdict within an hour.

"She's quiet and I don't think she trusts me, but outside of
that, she's not all that different."

Thus Joyce reported on their guest during the first two days Lydia Hopkins was in the house.

Lydia came upstairs for long, private conversations with Emtee Dempsey in the study, and the first night the old nun went downstairs to watch the evening news with Lydia.

"A bad idea," Joyce said. "They are still running sensational stories on the poor girl."

The poor girl! Kim thought this was going altogether too far. It was one thing to show Christian charity to a woman who had murdered her husband and daughter, but to suggest that Lydia was a victim called for an answer. Emtee Dempsey looked unblinkingly at Kim when she blurted this out.

"But, Sister Kimberly, she did not do those dreadful things."

"A jury thought she did."

"And now a judge has let her go."

"On a technicality. She hasn't been proved innocent."

"But if the trial was flawed she reverts to the state of innocence. It is *guilt* that must be proved, Sister."

"Yes, Sister."

"You're upset."

"No, I am not upset."

But of course she was. She felt like a child, peeved because someone else was receiving all the attention, peeved because Emtee Dempsey had excluded her from this latest venture in credulity. Maybe it wouldn't have been so bad if she had felt like an accomplice. Joyce fed Lydia and had something approaching conversations with her. Emtee Dempsey had spent at least twelve hours in all with the freed prisoner. Only Kim was left out.

"You might go down and keep her company, Sister Kimberly."

11

Kim nodded, suddenly flustered to have her bluff called. Joyce said, "I don't think she minds being alone. Maybe that's an effect of being in prison."

"On the contrary," Emtee Dempsey said. "Privacy and solitude are the last things she was permitted there. She was a specimen in a cage, someone to be watched. No, I think the peace and isolation of this house are just what she needs. She promised herself that if she were ever freed she would spend the rest of her life in prayerful solitude."

"That's us, all right," Joyce said.

Sister Mary Teresa took umbrage at this view of their religious life. "We should measure our life by the rule the Blessed Abigail wrote, not with reference to the Trappistines, Carmelites, or Carthusians. Ours is an orderly, recollected life of prayer."

Maybe it was, in its way. They began and ended each day in the chapel, saying the hours of the Little Office. They attended Mass daily. Since they did not have a chaplain, they walked or drove to the cathedral for Mass. Rarely, a priest would come to them and say Mass in their lovely if miniature chapel. Just thinking of their life here in a house designed by Frank Lloyd Wright, the gift of a grateful alumna, Kim realized how content she was with it. How silly to resent the kindness Emtee Dempsey was showing Lydia Hopkins.

That afternoon, Kim took coffee and cookies downstairs. The door of the apartment was open. Lydia Hopkins was seated at a little desk, her hands flat on the surface, her eyes closed. She might have been asleep. She might have been praying. Kim cleared her throat.

Lydia Hopkins's eyes were those of a surprised cat, not yet sure if it is in danger.

"I'm Sister Kimberly. I answered the door when you came."

Lydia nodded. Her eyes fell to the tray Kim held.

12

"Do you always eat so much?"

Kim smiled. "Joyce is a compulsive cook. These are oatmeal cookies."

"With raisins?"

"With raisins."

Lydia moved to the couch when Kim put the tray on the coffee table. "I thought I'd have tea with you, all right?"

A film formed over her greenish eyes. "I am having tea with you."

Kim sensed it would be wrong to insist that the apartment was Lydia's, that she could receive or not whomever she wanted there. She sensed that Lydia would not have believed it. She didn't quite believe it herself.

"How do you like this apartment?"

"To me it is luxurious."

"Do you need anything? This house is full of books."

"So Sister Mary Teresa said. For now, just being alone and able to think my own thoughts is like heaven."

"There's a chapel."

Lydia nodded. "I wasn't praying when you came in."

"Oh?"

"It was what I tried to do in prison. Just make a blank of my mind. A white screen. Nothing at all. I close my eyes and stare at the whiteness."

"It sounds a bit like meditation."

Lydia ignored that. "Pictures form of their own accord." She looked at Kim. "That's the problem."

"Do you want to talk about it?"

"Do you want to listen?"

"Of course."

"Of course?" A smile formed on her narrow mouth. Kim felt caught in a lie. Is politeness a lie? The prospect of hearing an account of those awful events in Elmhurst, and from Lydia Hopkins herself, had a certain morbid appeal.

13

But Kim would not have been disappointed if Lydia had said nothing.

Lydia said, "When I was seven years old I told a lie. I blamed another girl for the loss of my scarf. I thought that would be the end of it, but my mother of course insisted that we go to the girl's house and get the scarf back. We didn't have much, but they were poor. I stood in their living room next to my mother and allowed that poor girl to be accused of stealing my scarf. She denied it. But her mother didn't believe her. She had caught her in lies before. A few days later, the girl brought a new scarf to our house. She never said anything to me about it. Maybe she came to believe she *had* stolen my scarf."

"Did you say anything to her?"

"No." Lydia put down the cookie she held, as if she had lost the right to eat it. "I don't suppose you ever told a lie."

Kim laughed.

"Sister Mary Teresa claims she was an inveterate liar before becoming a nun."

"Then she's still at it," Kim said. "She can stretch the truth, anyway."

"She's wonderful."

"Yes."

They sat in silence for a while, then Lydia began to speak again, as if reciting words she had first formed in her head. "When I was in high school I was on the honor board. I stole a copy of the Spanish exam and the loss was discovered. Another girl was accused and she was brought before the honor board. I was the only one who knew she was innocent."

"Except her?"

"She ended up confessing. We all felt so sorry for her, we let her off easy." Lydia narrowed her eyes. "These are things I have never told anyone."

"Have you told them to Emtee Dempsey?"

14

"Emtee Dempsey?"

"It's what we call Sister Mary Teresa. Her initials."

Lydia smiled. "What are your initials?"

"K.O. Kimberly Olive. And Joyce is J.R. Do you know the program?"

"I would be Elsie, I guess. Lydia Catherine. Is there a Saint Elsie? If there is, I would like to take her name."

"Lydia is a lovely name."

"Have you ever thought that life is made up of smaller versions of itself? I have other stories like those I told. They are why I felt guilty during the trial. Not of . . . not of what I was accused. I felt I had been preparing myself all my life to be accused of something I had not done. I have put others in that position. And while I was being tried, during all these years, I felt I was being justly punished."

"For something you didn't do?"

"For something I didn't do."

There. She had said it. And Kim found it difficult to think Lydia was lying. Was it possible that all that evidence had not meant what it seemed to mean?"

"Well, now it is over."

"I hope you're right."

The next morning, Lydia walked to the cathedral with them. She wore a cape of Emtee Dempsey's and a scarf babushkalike over her head. She looked more like a nun than Kim and Joyce.

"Don't call her Lydia," Emtee Dempsey warned when they left the house.

"We'll call her Elsie," Kim said.

"Elsie!"

"My initials, Sister Mary Teresa," Lydia explained.

The old nun looked darkly at Kim. "What an inventive idea."

*　*　*

On the third day after Lydia's release from prison the voice of Manuel Carrillo was heard again in the land. The former prosecutor had been holidaying in Buenos Aires and news of the judge's decision did not reach him until he landed in Miami. No amount of jet lag could have prevented him from putting a call through to Chicago, demanding that he be assigned the task of conducting the new trial. Told that no decision had not yet been reached whether to try Lydia again, Carrillo's Latin rage exploded. He then telephoned his old friend Katherine Senski on the *Tribune*, and the early-morning editions carried the story. Manuel Carrillo had volunteered to prosecute Lydia once more. *After* he had made an effort to get the judge's opinion set aside by the full court. Since that seemed unlikely, he was already concentrating on the retrial.

The story had the effect Carrillo wanted. No one in the prosecutor's office had the stomach for further delay. For a few unreal days it had seemed possible that Lydia's release could be attributed to the incompetence of prosecutors of an earlier time, to the whimsicality of Judge Marsha Hunter—to anything but the current crop of prosecutors. They had been counting on the hullabaloo to rage itself into silence and that would be that.

But now Raymond Monday, the present prosecutor, spoke sternly to the cameras of his decision to seek a new trial.

Would he bring back Manuel Carrillo to conduct the prosecution? Although he must have expected the question, Monday could not conceal his annoyance.

"I don't intend to use the taxpayers' money in such a way that another technicality will undo our work."

Did that mean he would conduct the case himself?

Monday's jaw rippled as he clenched his teeth. "You

16

know the old saying about if you want something done right."

"Do it yourself?"

"That's the idea."

If Manuel Carrillo had been enraged by the judge's decision, Monday's suggestion that it was his incompetence that explained Lydia's release was too much. A copy of the *Tribune* in one hand, a box of popcorn in the other, he swept through O'Hare trailed by reporters who were intent on fomenting a feud. What did Carrillo think of Monday?

"He's a fine lawyer, no matter what people say. Lots of fine lawyers have trouble passing the bar exams."

A low blow perhaps, but one that had been first dealt by Monday's opponent when he was elected. The prosecutor had taken the bar exams twice in Illinois before passing them successfully and it was discovered that he had first tried the Florida exams and failed those.

"Any comment on Judge Hunter?"

"Her future is all ahead of her."

"Then you don't object to her judgment that the Lydia Hopkins trial was flawed?"

"I'll leave that to the full court to decide."

"Do you think they'll set it aside?"

"No, I don't. I think there will be a new trial. I want to conduct it." He stopped and shook some popcorn into his mouth and then, glaring at the reporters, said, "I am volunteering my services. Free. No taxpayers' money will be wasted putting a woman who brutally murdered her husband and child back in prison, where she belongs."

And then he asked a question that was to control the events of the next several days.

"Where is Lydia Hopkins now? Has she left the country? Does the prosecutor's office or the police even know where she is? Have any of you interviewed her?"

17

Of course none of them had. There was so much information on the murders and trial that it had seemed the story could be more than adequately covered without wondering where the released Lydia presently was. In several stories she was said to be in seclusion, which was simply a way of saying the writer did not know her whereabouts. But the shaming reality was that none of them had really cared, no one had thought to ask. Clearly it was time to blame the prosecutor for their own lack of curiosity.

WHERE IS LYDIA HOPKINS?

A banner headline that, the story revealed, was meant to underscore the heart of the interview with Manuel Carrillo. But there was little doubt that the question was directed at Prosecutor Monday.

Who immediately made querulous demands of the police. Where is Lydia Hopkins?

And so it was that Richard Moriarity, Kim's brother, received the task of finding the released prisoner and, after a fruitless forty-eight-hour search, dropped by the house on Walton Street to avoid reporters and unburden his woes.

It was not the first time that Richard had visited the house when, unbeknown to him, the person he sought was hidden on the premises, and as usual in such situations Kim felt pulled between loyalty to her brother and loyalty to her sisters in religion. Lydia waited in the study while Emtee Dempsey got Richard comfortable in the living room, then slipped down to the basement apartment, out of harm's way.

"You have a warrant for her arrest?"

Richard nodded. "If Monday knew what he wanted, we could have picked her up when she walked out of prison. But for days, she has been back to her status as ordinary citizen. Carrillo is right. She could be halfway around the world by now. She could be on the moon. She was free to do anything she wanted, legally. But now Monday puts the monkey on us, as if it was our fault she was given days in which to disappear."

"Any leads?"

Richard sipped the beer Joyce had brought him. "William Dunning picked her up and drove her to Chicago."

"Then he must know where Lydia is."

"If he does, he isn't telling me. I have someone keeping an eye on Dunning, of course."

"Phone calls?"

Richard shrugged. That meant yes, they were tapping Dunning's phone.

"Has she contacted Dunning?"

It was like watching a cat play with a mouse. Emtee Dempsey would justify her remarks by saying they were exactly what she would have said if she herself did not know where Lydia was.

"The warden says Lydia wrote to you, Sister Mary Teresa."

"Yes, she did."

Kim felt proud of Richard until she thought of Lydia downstairs.

"I don't suppose she's gotten in touch with you, has she?"

Emtee Dempsey gave him a chiding smile. "I think I know you well enough to be certain you would not have to ask me that question if she had."

The convoluted syntax, plus the implied flattery of the remark, got the old nun past this difficult moment.

Richard had three bottles of beer before he left, much to Kim's annoyance. He should be careful of drinking, he knew that. The Irish weakness ran in the family and Richard had too many responsibilities to run the risk. Of course she was equally annoyed with Emtee Dempsey for plying Richard with drink.

But one thing was clear. They were now harboring someone sought by the police, once more accused of two brutal murders, and facing a new trial on those charges. Even the practice of giving sanctuary has its constraints, and Kim felt certain they should feel them.

They discussed it in Emtee Dempsey's study—Kim, Joyce, the old nun, and the object of their collective concern, Lydia Hopkins. For the first time, Lydia's veneer of calm was removed.

"I can't stand the thought of going through all that again." She spoke through clenched teeth, her eyes closed. She hugged herself with both arms. In body language she was a person under siege. It was difficult not to feel compassion for her.

"Of course you needn't go through it," Emtee Dempsey said emphatically.

"But they want to arrest me."

"You're safe here."

Kim felt constrained to tell Sister Mary Teresa that they ran a risk harboring someone wanted by the law.

"Why can't Lydia reveal her whereabouts and then Mr. Rush can arrange bail?"

"Was bail permitted before?" Emtee Dempsey asked Lydia.

"No."

"Then it is doubtful it will be now. If anything, the hounds are more stirred up than ever. How can you expect a fair trial in this atmosphere?"

"Shouldn't we consult Mr. Rush?" Kim persisted.

"No. No, I think not. There is no need to put our old friend in an equivocal position. As an officer of the court, he would not want to know Lydia is here."

"Do you really want to join our community?" Joyce asked Lydia. Clearly she liked the thought of thwarting the law.

"I'm not sure," Lydia said. "I had such a romantic picture of what a convent would be like."

Kim could imagine the picture Lydia had formed in prison, dreaming of convent life. A choir, a community all dressed in habits, a building unlike this house on Walton Street. Reality was always a bit of a shock after daydreaming, and Lydia had the added factor of impending arrest to confuse her further.

After a pause, Sister Emtee Dempsey spoke. "I have decided to admit Lydia as a postulant. She needs at least six months of sharing our life before she can make an intelligent decision. Sister Joyce, you will make postulant's garb of the traditional sort. During this trial period, we will refer to Lydia as Elsie." She looked around. "In keeping with a tradition of this house."

The traditional postulant's habit was a daunting costume, although not as outrageously otherworldly as the garb Emtee Dempsey wore, with its full skirt, large starched wimple, and gull-shaped headdress.

"What about the police?" Kim asked.

"The police?"

"Sister, they will be searching everywhere for Lydia Hopkins. When—if—they find her, she will be arrested and put on trial."

Emtee Dempsey conceded the point with some reluctance.

"I don't suppose we can expect them simply to forget her."

"No."

In Kim's eyes an image of the body bags being carried from the house in Elmhurst formed. How often had that clip been shown on television? There was no chance in the world that the police would forget about Lydia Hopkins. The police. That meant Richard.

"Admittedly that complicates our task."

"You can't mean we will hide Lydia—"

"Elsie."

"—for an indefinite time."

"Like Anne Frank."

Anne Frank! But she was an innocent girl. Try as she would, Kim could not believe that Lydia Hopkins had not killed her husband and daughter. But she could not quite believe she had either. It was not a question she wanted to decide. Only a trial could produce a trustworthy verdict. She was thinking as a mere mortal of course. Emtee Dempsey had neither doubts nor scruples.

"Lydia is innocent," she pronounced. "I am as sure of that as I am of anything in this world. There is only one solution."

An expectant silence formed, but Emtee Dempsey seemed unaware of it. She had made a decision and that was that.

"What is the one solution?" Joyce asked.

"I will have to produce the person who killed Lydia's husband and daughter. That is the only way she will be left in peace."

Two

ister Mary Teresa's hubris was not surprising. Kim
might even have found it as attractive as Joyce apparently did if she had not known she would be pressed
into service to help Emtee Dempsey make good her boast.
The following morning, she was given a preliminary list of
things to be done, set down in random order.

1. Kim should speak to William Dunning, the lawyer,
and find what grounds he felt there were for Lydia's innocence. These must inevitably point in the direction of the
true murderer.

2. She was to interview all of Lydia's neighbors, particularly those who had played a role in the trial. Kim
was to discuss strategy and tactics in this regard with
Lydia.

3. Find out if Lydia was jealous of her husband. ("Jealousy?" "Remember the counteraccusation at the country

club?" "How can I find out a thing like that?" "I will ask Lydia.")

4. Interview employees of the country club.

"Anything else?" Kim asked, trying to keep sarcasm out of her voice.

"That will do for now. I am going to enlist Katherine Senski's help. She will be useful in getting access to crucial documentation."

"Such as?"

"She will be able to get us copies of all the videotapes that exist on this matter."

"You think you will find a clue on film shown to the public a zillion times?"

"Perhaps."

"Sister, these events took place years ago."

"No one is less likely to throw out any portion of the fruit of his efforts than a journalist."

"I'll tell Katherine you said so."

"It is Katherine I have particularly in mind. She has notebooks dating from her first days as a reporter. I am certain the libraries of TV studios will be jammed with interesting items."

"I hope so. I don't want you counting on me to prove Lydia innocent."

Emtee Dempsey shook her head in a reproving way. "Our task is to prove someone guilty, my dear. Lydia is as innocent as you and I."

"I'll try to keep that in mind."

"Do."

Like Emtee Dempsey, Katherine Senski was a woman of an age—a better age, as she might have said. She and Sister Mary Teresa Dempsey were battle scarred. As a member of the board of trustees of the college operated by

24

the Order of Martha and Mary, Katherine had been the old nun's main ally in their doomed effort to prevent the closing of the college and the selling of the grounds and buildings. The nuns who had been so eager to do more relevant work had metamorphosed right out of the religious life. The house on Walton Street and a summer place in Indiana were all that remained of a once-thriving religious order. The proceeds from the sale of the college had gone to the poor, and to setting up the now modishly dressed members of the order as bachelor gals.

But if they were old allies, it was clear that Katherine did not share Emtee Dempsey's view of Lydia Hopkins.

"She is far too sanguine," Katherine said to Kim, then winced. "Unfortunately, that is the *mot juste.*"

"Do you think you can change her mind?"

Katherine arched a brow. "And be accused of wanting to throw an innocent woman to the lions? Not on your life. No, there is only way to proceed."

"You sound like Emtee Dempsey."

Katherine smiled, revealing long teeth. Her nose was of noble size and her large eyes were pouched. It took a stronger imagination than Kim's to think of Katherine as attractive. Distinguished, yes, handsome even, but she could never have been beautiful, even pretty in a standard way. Emtee Dempsey said simply that Katherine had always been an attractive woman. But she would not discuss with Kim the tragic love that had marked Katherine's life, condemning her to the single state as surely as religious vows would have done.

The man had been older than Katherine, the attraction had been immediate and mutual, that odd chemistry between a man and woman that is activated by a congeries of accidents: a gesture that is vaguely reminiscent, the way eyes lift to meet one's own, the tone of the complexion, a trick of lighting—accidents, far from being the essence of anyone, but nonetheless what is operative when people fall in love. The remarkable thing is that it so often signifies a more profound affinity. Katherine and the older man had felt the initial irrational attraction; they learned that it revealed a deeper magnetism on both sides. In other circumstances, this would have led to marriage, a family, a life together. Alas, he already had a wife. Neither was capable of an affair; that would have seemed a parody of what they both wanted. And could not have. They agreed that they would only be friends. And so they had been. But it had doomed Katherine to the single life.

How could Kim and Joyce not want to know more, although what beyond these simple facts they expected to hear was difficult to say. It became the central fact about Katherine Senski. Her long career as the first woman of Chicago journalism, the prizes and awards she had received, her obvious intelligence and wit as she conversed with Emtee Dempsey—all that paled to insignificance beside the fact that Katherine Senski was a tragic romantic figure.

"Sister Mary Teresa wishes to find out who killed Jeffrey Hopkins and his daughter, Laura. Very well, I shall cooperate in every way."

"Do *you* think Lydia is innocent?"

"I didn't say that," Katherine said, giving Kim a long look. "Sister Mary Teresa may not be a happy woman when she satisfies her curiosity."

"Meanwhile, we hide Lydia?"

"Sister, I don't think it'll take very long to remove whatever doubts Sister Mary Teresa has about Lydia Hopkins's guilt."

Katherine's phone rang and she answered it. Whatever it was it was bad news, given the groaning with which it was received.

"Of course you'll have to print it," Katherine said indignantly, frowning at Kim as if she had suggested it.

"What is it?" Kim asked, when Katherine had hung up.

"Our mutual friend has made a public announcement that Lydia Hopkins is innocent. Moreover, she intends to prove it so that the poor woman will be left in peace."

An enterprising reporter, hearing that the old nun had corresponded with Lydia in prison, had called Walton Street and elicited the statement from Sister Mary Teresa. It made their own task more difficult. Were they trying to disprove Emtee Dempsey's claim or, against all the evidence and their own feelings, show that the old nun was right?

"Let the chips fall where they may," Katherine said, after a moment. "She wants to find out who killed Lydia's husband and daughter. Very well. We will help her."

So it was that Katherine lent her formidable knowledge and intelligence to the task of reviewing the evidence. One of her many prizes had been awarded as the result of her coverage of the Elmhurst Massacre, as Katherine's newspaper invariably referred to it. Thus she had a sizable file. Her notebooks she had indeed kept. And she had access to whatever the *Tribune* and its sister television station had on the case. But they agreed that Kim should begin by talking with the neighbors.

"Chiefly Mrs. Hughes across the street."

Driving past the house in Elmhurst, Kim could not help wondering what the double murder had done to property values in the neighborhood. Not that there was anything distinctive about the houses surrounding the one in which Jeffrey Hopkins and Little Laura had been brutally killed. It was just the sort of unlikely setting one has come to expect for such horrible deeds—a side road looking like

27

any other, a grassy hill beside a freeway where the sniper lies in ambush, a mobile home in a park with tricycles and wagons in the streets, this ordinary trilevel in Elmhurst.

With the help of Lydia, Kim had prepared a rough map of the neighborhood. It had been hard for Lydia to do, yet easy as well. The strained expression did not prevent her from giving quite specific help.

"In prison I would lie awake and stare at the concrete ceiling and try not to think of it, but it was always there. We had a seven-and-a-half-percent mortgage on the house. It would have been paid off in . . ." She stopped, and bit her lip.

"Do you still own it?"

"Bill Dunning tried to sell it but no one wants a murder house. But that was changing. If I had sold it before all this commotion, I would have made a very good profit. Now it's back to being a murder house again."

Across the street from the house lived Mrs. Hughes, the neighbor who had been so informative at the trial. Kim pulled the VW bug into the driveway and waited before getting out of the car. The division of the drapes widened slightly, then closed. So Mrs. Hughes was at home.

The woman's mahogany-colored hair was twisted into curls; there was a prominent mole on her cheek that seemed a parody of a beauty mark. She had the look of a soul lost in the crowd on some petty level of the *Purgatorio*. The face as mirror of the soul? A dubious doctrine, but it was difficult not to see in the petulant mouth, the wary yet somehow defiant expression, the dyed hair and puffy cheeks, outward signs of a resentful, self-pitying interior.

"Are you with the police?"

"No."

When she smiled, it was her lower teeth that were revealed, as in a man's smile. It seemed to suggest she and Kim understood one another.

"A reporter?"

Kim nodded, having difficulty not crossing her fingers. But Katherine had solemnly deputized her, claiming journalistic rights to anything Kim might come across, and so Kim stood on Mrs. Hughes's doorstep as, by extension at least, a representative of the press.

"What paper?"

"The *Tribune*."

"They've already been."

Kim nodded. "I'm working on a feature."

Visions of fugitive fame danced in Mrs. Hughes's eyes. The prospect of diverting for a minute or two newspaper readers, competing with advertisements, distractions, the lurch of a train, the roar and mumble and rhythms of daily life, melted any reluctance Mrs. Hughes might have had.

"Come in."

The living room was a battle scene where different styles of furniture competed to depress the spirit. Danish, Colonial, overstuffed, leather and cloth and brocade, lamps with bulbous plastic superstructures, others with fringed shades, and a bogus Tiffany that bore unmistakably the logo of a Milwaukee beer.

"It's crowded but I like it," Mrs. Hughes said with pride in her voice. "My sister left me her furniture."

Apparently, she had just added it to her own. The sister was gone to the actual purgatory, doubtless doing penance for her lack of taste. The surfaces of the tables were covered with figurines and gewgaws: a glass-enclosed winter scene, a letter opener whose handle bore the carved faces of Mount Rushmore, nests of ashtrays, wooden and

29

leather boxes—a riot of objects, none of which pleased the eye. Mrs. Hughes seemed to expect a comment.

"It's a remarkable room."

"I like it."

Several dozen volumes of *Readers Digest Condensed Books* occupied one shelf of a bookcase that also contained a small TV set. There was a large console model in the corner.

"I'm a widow." Her case against the universe.

"I see."

She laughed uncertainly. "One paper paid me for an interview?"

"How much?"

Mrs. Hughes's mouth opened but shut again before she spoke.

Kim said, "I don't consider that ethical."

"I took the money, don't worry about that."

"Well . . ."

"What kind of a feature are you thinking of?"

They sidled through the furniture to sit on facing wing chairs.

"That depends."

"I've already told everything I know." She added hurriedly, "But they didn't use everything. You talk for an hour and more and all they use is a few words."

"The murders occurred a long time ago, of course."

"It seems like yesterday to me. It seems like this morning. You don't forget a thing like that."

She was on now, aware that this was her claim to attention. Kim took notes, feeling like an impostor.

It was the major item in her repertoire and it would have been strange if Mrs. Hughes's account did not have a rehearsed quality. This is how she must have sounded reciting lessons as a girl in school: the tone of her voice not quite natural, speaking in a rush as if fearful of forgetting.

30

Mrs. Hughes had become aware of the dissension in the house across the street. In summer angry voices carried across to her. One or the other of the Hopkinses would eventually storm from the house and go for a walk or, more likely, get into a car and roar away.

"Taking the little girl with them. The one that got the girl won the argument, that's how it struck me. The poor little thing. Them always fighting and then her being snatched up and taken away by one or the other. What would she have been like if she lived, being brought up like that?" A borrowed theory of upbringing swam uncertainly in Mrs. Hughes's eyes as she looked over her half glasses at Kim. Kim did not encourage the threatening digression.

"Who has been living there?"

"That's the thing! It's still empty. They wanted to board up the windows, but we neighbors wouldn't have stood for that. When I was a girl, there was always a house we thought of as haunted. That house is." Her shoulder dipped in the direction of the Hopkins trilevel. But the drapes were still pulled, the console TV murmured unheeded inanities in the corner. It might have been on in order to prove that there was something beyond this jammed, closed room.

"Who would want to live in a house where things like that had happened? Oh, it's been kept up. A crew comes to do the lawn. Just the lawn. No flowers, nothing that needs real care. It would be a blessing if it burned down. I'm surprised some kid hasn't thought of that. The drapes? I keep them closed so I don't have to see that house and be reminded." Mrs. Hughes shuddered theatrically. "You going to use pictures?"

She didn't mean the house. Kim realized Mrs. Hughes was upping her bid for immortality. "I have a recent one I could give you."

31

"That would be helpful."

Mrs. Hughes rose immediately and managed to squeeze out of the room. Kim looked at the pulled drapes, at the TV that seemed to be beaming in evidence against an incredible civilization. People in what is called the world profess to pity the confined existence of the religious. Was any convent cell as penitential as Mrs. Hughes's living room in Elmhurst?

The worst part about such thoughts was that they brought in their wake shame for thinking them. Kim had no right to feel such condescension toward Mrs. Hughes. Emtee Dempsey would have reminded her that God loves Mrs. Hughes. After all, it is the Mrs. Hugheses Our Lord came to save. The not-so-imaginary conversation went on and the Emtee Dempsey in Kim's head ended with an admonishment. "We are all Mrs. Hugheses, Sister Kimberly."

A chastening thought. The picture was a travesty of a glamour shot. Lots of back lighting, Mrs. Hughes with chin uptilted, smiling seductively into the camera. Did she have hopes of altering her widow's status? How old was she?

Kim put the photograph in her purse. "I'll return it."

Mrs. Hughes watched her image disappear. "It was a premium. That's why I had it taken. I'm not sure I like it."

"Oh, you should. Mrs. Hughes, please go over the timing of those events. You were very definite about the time Lydia Hopkins left the house that day."

"It was just after two."

"You're sure?"

"That's my only vice." She meant the TV. "I always have it on. It's company of a kind. In the kitchen, the radio is never off. WBBM. They always give you the time. When I saw her come out and drive away, I was surprised she didn't have the daughter with her. I went into the

32

kitchen, so I could look out the side door. Come, I'll show you."

The kitchen seemed empty after the living room. Here everything was built snugly into the walls. A small table stood in a corner under a window, but the main area of the room was free. Mrs. Hughes had opened the kitchen door and was motioning Kim to come. From this vantage point, only a corner of the Hopkins house was visible.

"But I can see the street. When she backed out, she came to a stop right there. I can still see her."

"How do you mean?"

"Her expression. I don't know how to describe it. I was never good at that sort of thing. I've thought of it often. She was crying and her mouth twisted in the strangest way, as if she were talking to herself maybe. She looked back at the house and then she looked this way. I backed away from the door and just then on the radio they gave the temperature and the time. You would have thought I already knew then something had happened. If I did I didn't know it. But the time stuck in my mind. 'The time in Chicago is two-O-something.' And then they switched to the weatherman."

There seemed no reason to doubt her. Could Mrs. Hughes distinguish now between the events of that long-ago day and the subsequent descriptions of it? Probably not. If Lydia had come out of the house after two, this would have been after the emergency number had been called and the call interrupted.

Kim then asked the question Emtee Dempsey had particularly insisted she put to Mrs. Hughes.

"How long was it before the first police car arrived?"

"Oh, it was right afterward."

"Exactly how long would you say?"

"A few minutes?"

"How long would you say I've been here?"

A half smile formed and went away. "A few minutes."

Kim smiled in turn. "But how many?"

"Ten? Fifteen? I really didn't notice the time when you came in."

Kim had been in the house for thirty-five minutes.

Was this what Emtee Dempsey wanted, a kind of measure by which to judge the accuracy of Mrs. Hughes's assessment of the passage of time? If she were vague about the immediate present, how reliable was her memory of three years ago?

"Maybe a little longer?"

Again Kim had the impression of a schoolgirl, one who seldom had the right answer and, when she did, was not all that sure.

"It doesn't matter," Kim said.

It seemed like a lawyer's trick, throwing dust in the eyes of the jury, discrediting a witness.

"Why should I remember exactly when you came?" Mrs. Hughes asked. "The other was different. All that fighting. It kept you jumping, not knowing what they might do. I guess we all expected unconsciously that they couldn't go on that way. Something had to give."

"What was he like?"

"Good-looking. A little lazy. He didn't even do the yard work. A man came once a week on a little motorbike and did everything. Jeff Hopkins made you think of a spoiled kid, not much smarter than the yardman."

"Women liked him?"

"Well, let's say he had an eye for women. He might not mow the grass—someone came to do that—but in the summer he was out in the yard a lot. Some women lose their sense of modesty when the weather gets hot. I can see him now, out in a lawn chair like he was watching a show."

"But there was nothing more?"

Mrs. Hughes looked slyly at Kim. "You wouldn't put something like that in the feature, would you?"

"I'd like it for background."

"Well, I always thought that if she had cause to complain about him, Maggie Loomis could have been it."

"Where does she live?"

"Good Lord, you're not going to ask her, are you?"

"Not just like that, no."

"But if she knows you've been here . . ."

"I never reveal sources."

Mrs. Hughes did not take visible comfort from this declaration of journalistic ethics.

"How about yourself? Did he ever bother you."

Mrs. Hughes giggled. "I told you he had a roving eye."

The implied flattery of the question made up for her apprehension about any visit Kim might make to Maggie Loomis. In the doorway, Mrs. Hughes asked, "Do you have any idea when the feature will appear?"

"I'm at the mercy of editors."

Mrs. Hughes nodded in understanding.

Behind the wheel of the VW, Kim looked at the Hopkinses' one-time home. She tried but could not find anything sinister in that suburban trilevel—brick, metal shutters, the roof sparkling in the sunlight. The absence of flowers struck her only because Mrs. Hughes had mentioned it. A yard service came weekly to trim the lawn. Somehow that suggested the tending of a grave. Kim put the car in gear and moved slowly down the street to the Loomises' ranch-style house.

A woman wearing very short shorts that emphasized her fleshy upper legs sat in a lawn chair on the garage apron. She dipped her head to look over the tops of opaque sunglasses when Kim came to a stop. There was a very large book open on her lap and she kept her chin down, watching Kim come up the drive. The sweatband she wore gave her the look of an American Indian until she pushed the glasses back on her head.

"Mrs. Loomis?"

"Yes?" The wary tone of a housewife who has been stung too often by callers whose designs on her purse had not been clear at first.

"Kimberly Moriarity from the *Tribune*."

"Oh, God, it's all starting up again."

"I'm sorry to bother you."

"Be my guest." She waved at another chair. Her manner and voice were reluctant but she was clearly eager to talk.

"I've been talking to Mrs. Hughes."

Mrs. Loomis laughed. "The Eyewitness? That's what we call her. We always thought she was keeping tabs on everyone but Lydia's trial gave us real proof. Unless she was making it all up."

"She said they fought a lot."

"Jeff and Lydia? Of course they did. They were married, weren't they? That's what marriage is, an organized quarrel. Hughesie's been a widow too long to remember."

"You knew them well?"

"We were neighbors."

"I supposed you've talked about it dozens of times?"

"Look, I don't claim to have seen anything the day it happened. It surprised the hell out of me, if you want to know the truth. To this day, I can't believe it happened."

"You don't think Lydia is guilty?"

"Just say I'm glad she's free."

"Because she's innocent?"

Mrs. Loomis brought her glasses down off the top of her head, then put them back. "I said I wasn't surprised. True enough. On the other hand, I'm surprised I haven't taken a power saw to Emil. Emil's my husband. Maybe the real surprise is that there aren't more killings." Ice clattered in her glass as she sipped.

"What are you reading?"

She tipped the book so Kim could read the title. A *Bracelet of Bright Hair*, in Gothic lettering. Kim caught a glimpse of a long-haired girl surrendering to a fierce-eyed man. Mrs. Loomis laughed. "In winter I read better things. Summer is for trash."

"Did you ever visit Lydia while she was in prison?"

The question startled her. "In prison!"

"She could receive visitors, couldn't she? Did any of the neighbors ever go see her?"

"We didn't!" Her tone was indignant, but she couldn't hold the mood. She narrowed her eyes. "I get it. Callous neighbors abandon falsely accused housewife. Is that the angle?"

"Have you seen her since she got out?"

"She hasn't called," Mrs. Loomis said sardonically.

"And you haven't called her."

"I'll tell you what. You get me her number and I'll call her."

"I'd rather you told me about her."

"Listen, there was more in your paper about her than I ever knew."

"Were they as bad as they were described?"

"Bad?"

"Unfaithful?"

Maggie Loomis restored her sunglasses to her nose. "You want something to drink?"

"Thank you."

"This is a spritzer." She stood and tugged at her shorts with one hand, holding her glass in the other.

"What's a spritzer?"

"Wine and soda. No? There's iced tea."

There was the sound of lawn mowers on the summer air and from far off, dimmed by distance and heat, the muffled roar of a freeway was audible. From the house next door came the sound of amplified rock music. But Kim's attention was caught and held by the bees that came and went from a hive under the eave of the Loomis garage. Flowers were brilliant in beds along the front of the house and seemed to be the destination of the bees. Maggie Loomis came out of the open door of the garage with two glasses in her hands.

"You have bees," Kim said, unable to keep anxiety out of her voice.

"They won't bother you. They're making honey." She handed Kim a glass and eased herself into her chair, seeming to lift her glass to her lips in the same motion. "Birds and bees, that's us. Oh, this used to be some neighborhood. Now we're all grown old and respectable. Or we're widowed like Hughsie."

"What was Jeff like?"

"What did she tell you?"

"She told me to ask you."

The glasses went up again. "You want to know what happened between Jeff Hopkins and me?"

"If you want to tell me."

"Nothing. I mean nothing serious. Kidding around, sure. It was a sort of standing joke. He and I were going to run away and live in sin together. That's the way he talked. Talked. I doubt that he ever *did* anything. A pat on the bottom, a kiss, sure, but always with others around. A game."

"Is that how Lydia saw it?"

Maggie's eye followed a bee as it executed a little dance and then went into the hive. "She was a very silly woman if she didn't."

"Do you think she killed her husband and daughter?"

38

"Sure I do."

"Why?"

"My God, all the evidence."

"That you read of in the papers? I mean on the basis of what you knew of her."

"Who else could have done it?"

"Good question."

"With a million answers. I mean, if not Lydia, then damned near anybody. No, not quite. Any wife probably thinks she has good reason to kill her husband."

"What did you think when you heard she was released from prison?"

"I thought, good for her. And why not? How many murderers spend much time in prison nowadays? I was glad."

"They want to bring her to trial again."

"A waste of taxpayers' money. Emil says they're only doing that so she doesn't sue the state, which she ought to do anyway."

"Is Emil a lawyer?"

She laughed. "Emil owns four franchise food drive-ins."

"Do you belong to the country club?"

"Are you kidding?"

"Then you don't."

"That was always a guessing game in this neighborhood, how could Jeff Hopkins afford a membership. Well, he inherited money. Or she did. Maybe both. But it wasn't on his salary. So why did they live here? Don't ask me. It must have been the birds and the bees." She laughed and took a drink.

Kim decided that Maggie Loomis had a pretty face, at least it must once have been. Now it was flushed and puffy. The tank top scarcely contained her and even without those absurd shorts it would have been clear that she had let herself go. Sitting here under the honey-making bees, reading A *Bracelet of Bright Hair*, sipping her mildly alcoholic drink, Maggie Loomis did not suggest a homebreaker. She tipped back her glasses when Kim rose to go.

"Please don't use my name in your story."

Kim nodded.

"Have *you* talked to Lydia?"

"Yes."

She sat forward. "Tell me about her."

"What do you want to know?"

"Is she bitter?"

"She is very subdued. And religious."

Maggie Loomis sat back, nodding, as if Kim had restored the order of the universe. "That figures."

"How do you mean?"

"Watergate."

"I don't understand."

"After you get caught, you get religion. Isn't that the pattern? Guilt can be profitable."

"She says she wants to become a nun."

Maggie Loomis's capacity for surprise had not been exhausted. Her mouth hung open. "Seriously?"

"Time will tell."

"But won't there be another trial?"

"That's what they say."

"I don't think either of them ever went to church. Jeff and Lydia. They were Catholics, but it didn't seem to matter." She put down her drink and stood. "I'll walk with you to your car. Where could I get in touch with Lydia?"

"I can tell her that you asked."

"So you'll be seeing her again."

"Yes."

"Tell her to call me."

Kim promised to deliver the message. The VW didn't start immediately and Kim sat in the hot car, smiling up at Maggie Loomis, who, arms crossed, stood beside the door.

Finally the motor caught and Kim waved and pulled away, driving up the street as Lydia had one February afternoon at a little after two. Kim was meeting Katherine Senski for lunch. Where had Lydia Hopkins gone when she drove away that day?

At the Pioneer Club, they were led to a table near the great window that looked out over the Art Institute toward Lake Michigan, Katherine sweeping among the diners as if she were driving the maître d' before her rather than following him. As with most of her dresses, the one Katherine now wore seemed to involve twice as much material as was necessary. It was silk and blue and beautiful, suggestive of a forgotten style, somehow perfect for Katherine. She put her notebook on the table, retained a hold on her massive purse, and permitted the man to help her get seated. Kim was already in the chair before the stuffy maître d' could assist her.

"Ralph, an executive martini, please. I can't wait for the waiter. It's been a dreadful morning."

He nodded and raised an eyebrow at Kim.

"A spritzer."

"A spritzer," he repeated and after a pause went away. Katherine was staring at Kim.

"A spritzer! Poor Ralph. you might as well have ordered a boilermaker. Wonderful." She patted Kim's hand.

"I've embarrassed you."

"Not at all. Where did you learn of spritzers?"

"Maggie Loomis."

"Aha. And what else did you learn?"

"Nothing I hadn't read in the papers."

Their drinks came, Katherine's in a flask embedded in a diminutive ice bucket. The glass put before Kim did not look like the one from which Maggie Loomis had sipped. The waiter identified it as a wine cooler and seemed to

41

want her approval. She nodded but he hovered until she sipped it.

"Sister Kimberly, you are not likely to stumble upon something that will exonerate Lydia Hopkins. There is no such thing. The woman is guilty as charged. If there is another trial, she will be found guilty again. Her main hope is that Raymond Monday will let her go in order to spite Manuel Carrillo. In the meantime, you need only report to our mutual friend that nothing has changed."

"She won't accept that."

"Not easily. She is stubborn but she is not irrational. She would much better devote her efforts to preventing a retrial. An argument could be made—though not by me—that the woman has suffered enough. Doubtless Sister Mary Teresa thinks it is sufficient punishment to have such a crime on one's conscience."

"*Agenbite of inwit.*"

"I beg your pardon."

"Remorse of conscience."

"You're getting as bad as your mentor. But you must deflect her from this quixotic goal. Lydia Hopkins murdered her husband and daughter. Brutally."

"Emtee Dempsey says she didn't. And Lydia denies it."

"She always did. You can count on the fingers of a mutilated hand the murderers who admit their crime."

"If you think Sister can be persuaded, you should try it yourself."

Katherine thought about it, looking out where sails moved like a problem in geometry over the sparkling water. "We will let the truth persuade her."

"Where did Lydia Hopkins go when she drove away from her house that February afternoon?"

Katherine flipped open the notebook she had brought and murmured half aloud as she read. She looked at Kim. "Apparently to the Elm Stand Town and Country Club.

But she wasn't arrested until the following morning at her lawyer's office."

"William Dunning?"

"Have you talked with him yet?"

"He hasn't had time for me yet."

"Has Lydia?"

"Not since she came to the house. Unless they have spoken on the telephone. I guess I really don't know. But after the club, where was she until the following morning?"

"I am sure Dunning can answer that. I cannot. She had been seen driving away from the house."

"By Mrs. Hughes."

"By the vigilant Mrs. Hughes. Once she surrendered, no one asked where she had been. I see that I did not. Except to find in that unaccounted-for period the explanation of why there was no blood on her or on her clothes. What she did after the killings paled into insignificance when her actions before them became known. That she was at the house. And that she was seen leaving."

Kim did not think these unaccounted-for hours were any more significant than Katherine did. But she could all too easily imagine Emtee Dempsey pouncing on any unknown and making it the heart of the matter.

She was wrong. The old nun had already asked the one person sure to know.

"She went from the club to her lawyer's. She spent that night in a motel because she had quarreled with her husband and had decided to leave him. The following morning, William Dunning told her what had happened and they called the police."

Emtee Dempsey sat at her desk and she did not put down her pen as she spoke.

43

Kim reported on her conversations with Mrs. Hughes and Maggie Loomis and on her lunch with Katherine.

"Katherine, of course, thinks I am mad," Emtee Dempsey said.

"Well, she thinks Lydia is guilty."

"She is wrong."

"She hopes so."

The old nun frowned and pursed her lips. It might have been a moment of self-doubt. Until she spoke.

"Public exoneration of guilt should be established before Elsie's profession."

Three

J ane Flannery sat sideways at her desk, her fingertips
touching the keyboard of a computer, a view of the
tennis courts of the Elm Stand Town & Country Club
framed in the window behind her. If she had rested her
chin on her shoulder she might have been parodying a fan
photo of a movie star of the sixties, which would have
been when she came of age.

"Sister Mary Teresa Dempsey called you," Kim said.

The thin-lipped mouth opened slightly and Jane Flannery swung in her chair to face Kim. "Are you . . . ?"

"Sister Kimberly."

The woman looked her up and down. "You could have
fooled me."

Kim smiled, hoping the remark was just a remark. If
Jane Flannery was ill-disposed toward nuns who did not
wear traditional habits, this trip had been in vain. "The
Order changed its mode of dress after the Council."

"You don't mean even Emtee Dempsey is now wearing double-knit pants suits."

Kim held her tongue. She herself had never worn a double-knit pants suit in her life. "Keeping the traditional habit was optional."

"And she kept it? Good for her. I don't know when I last saw her. We talk on the phone but only from time to time."

"You knew Lydia Hopkins, didn't you?"

"So that's what this is about." Jane Flannery's fingers tapped on the braided hair that wound around her head. It might have been another computer keyboard. "What's Sister's interest in Lydia Hopkins? Apart from the fact that she's in all the papers again, that is."

"She intends to prove her innocent."

Jane could not quite stifle a skeptical laugh. She shook her head. "I read what Sister said in the paper. It can't be done."

"You think she's guilty?"

"*Think* she's guilty! She was tried and convicted and sent to prison."

"But now she's out again."

"A fluke. They'll convict her again, on the same evidence."

"What was she like?"

"Did Emtee Dempsey just read about her in the paper and decide she was innocent?"

"They corresponded while Lydia was in prison."

"Have they ever met face to face?"

Kim did not want to lie. One of the worst things about doing such errands for Emtee Dempsey was that she always seemed on the verge of telling a lie or, if not actually lying, misleading people in ways that are worse than lying.

"Why do you ask?"

"All she has to do is spend an hour or two with Lydia and she'll know."

"She doesn't think so. Tell me about Lydia."

Jane Flannery made a quarter turn in her chair and looked almost wistfully at the screen of her computer, where a spreadsheet was in evidence. She had been business manager of the Elm Stand Town & Country Club since her husband died.

"Even before," Emtee Dempsey told Kim before sending her off to obtain such information as Jane Flannery could provide about the Hopkinses during the few years they had been members of the club. Jane Witta married Lloyd Flannery a month after graduating from the college the Sisters of Martha and Mary had operated in a western suburb. Lloyd had gone through Notre Dame in ROTC and was soon on his way to Vietnam. He never returned. He was buried in Arlington and years later Jane looked for and found his name on the black marble memorial. Jane was working in the office at Elm Stand Town & Country when the telegram came and she had been working there ever since.

Now Jane punched a button and the screen of her computer went blank. For a moment more she stared at the dark rectangle. Beyond her the canvas attached to the tennis court fence flapped in the breeze. Then once more she turned toward Kim.

"How about some coffee?"

There was a coffee maker on top of one of the file cabinets. Jane closed the door to the outer office after she had filled their cups. Back behind her desk, she sipped from her cup and began to talk. She talked uninterruptedly for twenty minutes. There was not a word in anything she said that offered the slightest support to Emtee Dempsey's assumption that Lydia Hopkins was innocent and had been wrongly convicted.

The first thing Jane Flannery emphasized was that Lydia used the country club as a baby-sitter. A day-care center. She would drop that lovely little girl off every day as soon as the pool opened for summer. Jane would see her do it from the window of her office. The car hardly stopped, just paused for little Laura to hop out with her canvas bag, and then off Lydia would go. As often as not it was the father who picked up the child late in the afternoon. Or worse, she would mope around the place in the summer twilight waiting for him to come in from the golf course.

"Let one time stand for them all." Jane paused, an odd smile on her face. "There's a word for that. I remember Sister Mary Teresa telling us."

"Synecdoche."

"Now I really believe you live with her. Anyway, one afternoon—it could have been one of hundreds—little Laura was here from maybe nine in the morning. She spent so much time in that pool she must have been puckered all over. She could swim like a fish and the life-guards liked her, but all day every day? A child senses things, I suppose, so she would leave the pool and wander around, as often as not still wearing her bathing suit, maybe spend half an hour or more on the practice putting green. And she was taking tennis lessons. This is a nice club and it may seem odd to feel sorry for the children of members. I do feel sorry for them, many of them, but Laura Hopkins was the most pathetic. Everyone pitied her and that made it worse, she knew that was what we were feeling. Well, the day I'm talking about she had lunch in the Cork Room, having dressed after swimming, and then about two Clara Monterone came by and told me Laura was curled up in a leather chair in the members' library and she didn't care what the rules were, she was going to let her stay.

"Mr. Hopkins golfed that afternoon, teeing off at four. It was nearly six when he finished the first nine and found Laura sitting on the patio when he came up to the clubhouse for a beer. Where was her mother? She didn't know. How long had she been at the club? All day. Well, he took her along on the back nine, letting her drive the cart. Lydia showed up and made a big thing of looking high and low for Laura. Someone told her she had been in the library and when Clara couldn't tell her where little Laura was now, she became hysterical, accusing Clara of negligence, dereliction of duty: it was unbelievable! In the pro shop, they told her Laura was out on the course with her father. Benny drove Lydia onto the course in his golf cart to pick up Laura. Apparently, she and Jeffrey had a real shouting match on the sixteenth fairway but soon Lydia returned to the clubhouse with Laura. The two of them were in the dining room when he finished his round. The shouting match started up again but Phyllis put an end to that. She is as much den mother as hostess and she doesn't want any domestic quarrels in her dining room. But she wasn't in time to prevent Jeffrey from accusing Lydia of spending the day with her lover and abandoning Laura."

The events Jane narrated had taken place years ago, but she recounted them with distaste and obvious dislike for Lydia Hopkins.

"*Did* she have a lover?"

"She might just as well have."

"What does that mean?"

"He thought so and nothing she could say could disprove it."

"But was it true?"

49

Jane hesitated but apparently won an argument with herself. "I don't know. I don't think so."

"Why?"

"I'm only guessing, but she wasn't the type. For one thing, she was a flirt."

"That's not the type?"

"Almost never. People who kid about fooling around seldom do."

"And she kidded about it?"

"She couldn't talk to a man without putting a hand on his arm. She leaned toward them when she spoke. She was a kisser too, both hello and good-bye. The women who have been unfaithful in this club, the ones I know about anyway, were all the serious type. They weren't playing around, they were in love, playing for keeps. Most of them divorced their husbands to marry the new man."

"How about him?"

"Jeffrey Hopkins?" Jane shrugged. "He was a man."

"Meaning yes?"

"Meaning that you couldn't really expect him to turn down an opportunity if it did not threaten unwelcome consequences."

"Isn't that cynical?"

"Maybe. Original cynical."

"Could I talk to Clara?"

"Sure, but she won't answer. She's gone to God. Cancer. Two years ago."

"I suppose there is an annual turnover in the life-guards."

"The old hands around here are three. Me, Fritz in the bar, and Phyllis. One more. Fenwick, the retired pro, lives in a condominium along the eleventh fairway."

"Is he the Benny you mentioned?"

Jane laughed. "No. Benny just works in the pro shop. He's not really grown up. No point in talking to Benny."

"Will the others talk to me?"

"Sure. Maybe not Fenwick. But try him anyway. He knew them both. He even liked them both."

Jane Flannery's attitude toward Lydia, the shrew she described, the clear indication that Lydia was everything she had been accused of being during her trial, shocked Kim. It was the Lydia of the newspaper stories she had been hearing about from Jane Flannery, not the woman who had been staying with them on Walton Street. The contrast between the negligent mother, shrewish wife, and possibly unfaithful spouse and the subdued, reflective woman in their basement apartment could not have been greater. But of course some years and the chastening effect of prison had intervened between the time of which Jane Flannery had spoken and now. And, if Lydia were guilty . . .

Kim stopped the thought. It had become a kind of disloyalty even to entertain the possibility. Besides, Emtee Dempsey had vowed to prove Lydia innocent by finding the one who really had killed her husband and child.

Why was the old nun so certain Lydia was innocent? But of course if she had had any basis for her certainty she would not have sent Kim to the country club to find what she could find.

"What am I looking for?" Kim had asked the night before when Emtee Dempsey renewed her assignment.

"That is what we don't know."

What she was not looking for was reason to think Lydia guilty, and so far that was all Kim had found.

There was a grill room on the lower level, its flooring impervious to the spiked shoes of golfers, windows looking out upon a practice green. The Cork Room. The grill could be entered from the green through French doors, from swinging doors that led into the locker rooms, from

51

the pro shop, and by way of the stairs, down which Kim had descended.

In midmorning, the chairs were still upended on the tables. A very tall, cadaverous-looking man in black trousers and a snow-white shirt stood on the customer side of the bar, reading a newspaper open before him, a cup of coffee held motionless before his face. He fit the description of Fritz she had been given by Jane Flannery. Kim told him who she was. He sipped his coffee and did not look at her.

"Want coffee?"

"No, thanks."

He shrugged. "Jane just called down." He glanced at her out of the corner of his eye.

"She said you were a nun."

"Yes."

"Are you?"

"Yes."

"What kind?"

She told him.

"Jane talks about you all the time."

"Not me, surely."

"No, an old nun."

"Sister Mary Teresa. I live with her. She's why I'm here."

"She wanna take up golf?" He chuckled softly at his joke.

"She thinks Lydia Hopkins is innocent."

"So I heard. On what basis?"

A reasonable enough question. But Kim didn't want to say that Emtee Dempsey just knew.

"Lydia says she is."

"Nothing changed there. And now she's out again. Don't we have a nice court system, though? A person duly tried, found guilty, sentenced, and then, after she's been in prison a couple years, some judge decides the trial was flawed."

"Imagine yourself in her place."

He finished his coffee. "You want a Coke or something, I can give you that."

"I had two cups of coffee with Jane Flannery."

"The restrooms are through there."

She took him up on it, pushing through into a wide hallway filled with the lingering smell of steam and soap and wet towels. Her step was soundless on the rubberized floor and she wended her way through the women's locker room feeling like an intruder.

Between two rows of lockers a woman wearing a billed cap and pleated skirt was tying her shoes. She smiled at Kim.

"Is it through here?"

"Straight ahead."

The woman was no longer in the locker room when Kim came back through again.

In the grill Fritz was taking chairs from the last of the tables. The room seemed bigger now. They sat at a round table in round-backed chairs, Kim facing the window and the practice green.

"Jane told me little Laura Hopkins used to spend hours on that green."

"Poor little kid. You get my age, you begin to think maybe she was better off dying young. But you would understand that."

Kim wasn't sure she did.

"Do you think Lydia killed her husband and daughter?"

"What difference does it make what I think? It doesn't seem to matter what a jury thought. Ask the judge, she seems to know everything."

"Neither the jury nor the judge could know what you do."

He had refilled his coffee cup and now seemed to consult its surface for a response.

He said, "Have you ever known a murderer?"

"Yes."

"I never have. So far as I know. What have I got to compare her with?"

"So she could be innocent?"

"I didn't say that."

Outside on the practice green the woman who had been tying her shoes in the locker room was lining up a putt. Kim marveled at the woman's concentration. How much time would she spend perfecting her ability to knock a little ball into a hole? But many jobs are as pointless as golf. Maybe it is why and how we do what we do rather than the activity itself that really matters. After all, Fritz's job consisted of making drinks that affected the nervous systems of his customers in such a way that their moods and outlooks were changed. Upstairs, Jane Flannery was busy keeping the books of a private club dedicated to the diversion of its members. And I, thought Kim, am here collecting gossip about Lydia Hopkins.

Fritz followed her gaze through the window. "That is Dolores Merrill. She's wasting her time."

"How do you mean?"

"She'll never be a better golfer than she is."

"I thought she was doing well."

"Some people practice well and play badly. Some are the reverse, but not Dolores Merrill."

"She just missed the hole."

"Maybe she will improve. Her husband has a one handicap."

"What does that mean?"

"He's very good. On the golf course. Off, that's something else." He looked at Kim. "You might ask Lydia about her."

"What's the connection with Lydia?"

"Ask her."

She might have admired him for not spreading gossip, but she was annoyed that he would not finish what he began. Not that she would beg him.

"Anything else I should ask Lydia?"

"Not that I can think of. I'm going to get some more coffee."

Kim rose. "Thanks for talking to me."

"Who else did Jane suggest you see?"

"Phyllis Bastable and Adam Fenwick."

He nodded. "Didn't she mention Bill Dunning?"

"Her lawyer?"

"Of course you'd already know about him."

Going back up the stairs from the grill, Kim wondered at the insinuating tone in which Fritz had made that last remark.

Phyllis, the hostess in the main dining room of the club, had some of the characteristics of the maître d' at Katherine's club until she understood who Kim was.

"Jane said you'd be dressed like that." Her smile suggested that Kim was out of uniform but Phyllis wouldn't tell. The hostess must have bought her clothes in the big-girl shops, if only to accommodate her massive if well-shaped bosom.

"Did she tell you why I'm here?"

A nod. "We can talk in here."

She meant a private dining room that was entered by a door just beyond Phyllis's pulpit desk, on which her appointment book was opened. She asked one of the waitresses to look after things, but it was scarcely after eleven and the dining room was empty.

"The Hennesseys will be in at eleven-fifteen as usual." To Kim she said, "They have brunch every day. Every day

55

eggs Benedict." She widened her mouth and stuck out her tongue. Despite the sprayed hair, the makeup, the lovely dress and haughty manner, Phyllis might have been Joyce in disguise. She even lit, furtively, a cigarette as soon as she closed the door of the smaller room. "So what can I tell you of our big scandal? That is what it was called around here at the time. But I think there are those who enjoy the fact that it's being dredged up again."

"Do you know Sister Mary Teresa?"

"Only by reputation. Jane is a great fan of hers."

"Sister Mary Teresa thinks Lydia Hopkins is innocent."

Bluish smoke rose sinuously from the filtered cigarette Phyllis held between red-tipped fingers.

"Does she know her?"

"They corresponded when Lydia was in prison."

"Pen pals?" She laughed and the fingers of her free hand briefly touched Kim's arm. "That can't be original."

"I've never heard it."

"Lydia killed them, her husband, her little girl. I don't know what she said to the nun, but she did it. Read the trial."

"I've read a great deal about it. Tell me about the ashtray."

The episode had been featured in Phyllis's testimony. They quarreled in the dining room, shouting, and, when Jeffrey was leaving, Lydia threw an ashtray at him.

"She missed. It was written up as a lethal weapon, which I doubt. The point of it was her anger. She was out of control. In public! Actually, I was in more danger than Jeffrey Hopkins. Her distance was better than her aim. That's how Fenwick put it. There was that kind of joking. Her backswing was too fast. She had hooked it. Golf talk. You expect that around here."

"What was the argument about?"

"They each thought the other was playing around."

"Anything to it?"

"On his side? Sure."

"Sure, or just rumor?"

"I don't have black-and-white glossies, if that's what you mean, but if he and Dolores Merrill weren't up to something, I'll join the convent myself."

"That's what Lydia wants to do."

"She ought to."

"How do you mean?"

"Do penance. I don't mean to sound smug. But if there is any justice, she should still be in prison. The way she treated that little girl. It was terrible."

"You don't go to prison for that."

"You do when you kill them."

Phyllis put out her cigarette, not displeased with her remark. "You serious about Lydia and the convent?"

"It's what I heard."

"Would you like lunch?"

"Not really."

"The stuffed tomato is out of this world. Shrimp. Practically no calories. Look."

She opened the menu she had brought with her, her badge of office, and showed Kim the dietary addenda to each of the items—calories and cholesterol and other menaces registered.

"How can I? I'm not a member."

"I'm inviting you."

But it was too early to eat just yet. Besides, Kim wanted Phyllis to talk more of the Hopkinses.

"A thing that didn't come out at the trial, I suppose they didn't need it, was the fact that he had hired a detective to follow her."

"Did he find anything?"

"That was the basis for the argument."

"I suppose the police checked that out."

57

"I suppose."

But it was of Little Laura Phyllis spoke most, that pathetic child wandering around the club all summer. "God knows what life was like for her during the rest of the year."

"Does the club close?" Kim asked, when they returned to the main dining room.

"No. But we might just as well. The dining room is the main attraction, out of season, but there are days . . . The Sunday brunch is well attended all year round, but some evenings you could shoot a cannon through the dining room and not hit anyone. Or throw an ashtray." She lit another cigarette. "Does this smoke bother you?"

"Not at all."

"Now we don't keep ashtrays on the tables." She had been using a saucer. "The waitress will bring one if asked, but the hope is that members will smoke outside the dining room. The smoking room has been brought back. It was part of the original design, apparently, but it was put to other uses. Now we have a smoking room to which addicts withdraw to smoke and talk about when they intend to quit. Isn't it a pain the way everything is a danger to your health? As if people wouldn't die if they took care of themselves. Jeffrey Hopkins didn't smoke." Phyllis said it as if it were Q.E.D.

The hostess put Kim at a small table and went away. There was an elderly couple in a corner and, near the window, sipping a drink, the woman Kim had seen earlier. Dolores Merrill. She asked the waitress, to make sure. After what Phyllis had said, it was hard not to stare at the woman. She had changed from golfing clothes into an organdy dress that seemed light as a feather. The light from the window gave her an ethereal look, turning her hair into spun gold, making her look much younger than she had seemed earlier. Phyllis stopped at the woman's table and said something, and then both turned toward Kim, who looked quickly away lest her eyes meet theirs. When she looked again, the woman was coming across the room to her table.

"If you want to know about Lydia Hopkins, you should ask those who know." The woman stood stiffly and her lips trembled as she spoke.

"That's what I'm trying to do. You're Dolores Merrill."

With a nod, she pulled out a chair and sat sideways on it across from Kim. She leaned forward and there was a strange intensity in her eyes. "Have you talked with Lydia since she got out of prison?"

"Yes."

"Where?"

"Why do you ask?"

"Because it terrifies me to think that woman is running around loose. What is she like now?"

"You're terrified?"

"She threatened me before. Did you know that? She wanted to kill me too."

Dolores Merrill rubbed her thumb back and forth on the handle of a spoon she had picked up.

"The Lydia Hopkins I talked with does not seem likely to threaten anyone."

"Well, the Lydia Hopkins I knew swore she would take care of me. She telephoned me from prison."

"Lydia telephoned you?"

"My fear was that she would hire someone to harm me. Now she can do it herself." She put down the spoon and aligned it carefully with a knife. "Tell her this. I have hired protection. I am never without someone watching me." She stood and looked down at Kim, as if about to say more, but then turned on her heel and left the dining room. A short, robust man who had been seated near Phyllis's station followed Dolores Merrill out.

59

"Sorry about Mrs. Merrill," Phyllis said as Kim was leaving.

"Who was that man who followed her?"

"The Hennessys' driver." Phyllis's eyes lifted. "Her driver. Dolores is a little nuts. Always has been. Once she was investigated for sending threatening letters to the president. Which she claimed she never wrote. She hasn't been the same since."

"She says Lydia Hopkins threatened her."

"Of that Lydia may have been innocent."

Driving back to Walton Street, Kim could understand that Dolores Merrill might have been encouraged in her fantasies after Jeffrey and Little Laura were so brutally killed. William Dunning was at the house when Kim arrived home, and she joined the lawyer and Sister Mary Teresa in the study.

Emtee Dempsey had applied to William Dunning Thomas Hardy's description of Damon Wildeve in *The Return of the Native*: "Altogether he was one in whom no man would have seen anything to admire, and in whom no woman would have seen anything to dislike." A lady's man, that is, "too good-looking by half," in the old nun's phrase, and possessed of an excellent if overly shrewd intelligence. Thus, on this occasion, aware that the police were expecting to be led by him to Lydia Hopkins's hiding place, he had made sure his client was out of the house on Walton Street before he came.

"We expect Richard at any moment," Emtee Dempsey said. "Are there questions you would like to put to Mr. Dunning, Sister?"

"Yes. Tell me about Dolores Merrill."

"She's crazy," Dunning replied then sat with a closed-lipped smile.

"She told me she was threatened by Lydia."

"She was. For propositioning Jeffrey."

60

"Is that true?"

"Jeffrey said so."

"Is it true that Lydia threatened her?"

Emtee Dempsey interrupted. "That is a question we can put to Lydia herself. What I want to know, Mr. Dunning, is whether or not Lydia will be retried."

He ran his index finger down his nose, over his upper lip, and let it rest on his chin. "I don't see how it can be avoided. Your earlier thought remains correct. The only way to deflect attention from Lydia is to come up with a plausible suspect."

"With the one who actually killed Jeffrey and Laura Hopkins," Emtee Dempsey corrected.

"That's what I meant."

"Mr. Dunning, you more than anyone else will have given thought to this matter. Who do you think killed those two people?"

Dunning looked theatrically over both shoulders. "I will say things here that I could not state publicly." He spoke directly to Kim. "How did Adam Fenwick strike you?"

"I haven't spoken with him yet."

"I urge you to. Within these walls, I will tell you that, if I had been the prosecutor, I would have wanted the focus on Fenwick."

"Who is Adam Fenwick?" Emtee Dempsey asked patiently.

"The golf pro at Elm Stand Town and Country Club." The old nun looked at Kim. "Sister?"

"He teaches people how to play golf and is paid to do so. Mr. Fenwick is now retired."

"Where does he live?"

"On the golf course." Kim added, when Emtee Dempsey lurched in surprise. "On the club grounds. There is housing that borders the golf course."

"Then you can speak to him. Mr. Dunning, is there

61

something that might be done to deflect interest onto Mr. Fenwick?"

"Not by me, I'm afraid. It would look too self-serving. Tell me, Sister Kimberly, has anyone you talked with provided a lead?"

"I'll let Sister Mary Teresa decide. After I've reported on those conversations."

The old nun liked that, although Kim was not sure why. Nothing whatsoever pointed to the likelihood that someone else might emerge as the slayer of Jeffrey and Laura Hopkins. Quite the contrary. Everything she had heard during the past two days had rocked Kim's willingness to take Lydia's word that she was innocent.

Emtee Dempsey said, "You might explain to Sister Kimberly why you came here this afternoon."

Dunning brought his hands together like a priest. "Of two things, we are going to have to do one. Either produce Lydia and hope that bail will be set, a hope which would not, alas, be firmly grounded in the present atmosphere, or continue to conceal her whereabouts in the hope that we can produce a plausible—produce the true killer. It was because I knew coming here would lead the police to the house that I wanted Lydia elsewhere during my visit. Incidentally, where is she?"

"It is best you don't know," Emtee Dempsey said sweetly.

"True. Nonetheless, I think my visit has made this house a less safe refuge for Lydia. If we take the second course, a safer permanent hiding place will be necessary and, as you correctly notice, one I must know nothing about. It is possible for me to admit being able to communicate with my client and still deny that I know where she is."

"There is no doubt at all which course we shall take," Emtee Dempsey said emphatically. "Lydia is now for all practical purposes a member of the Order of Martha and Mary and deserving of our protection, but even if she had simply sought sanctuary with us, I would refuse to turn her over to the tender mercies of Mr. Monday."

Kim listened with a sinking heart, knowing she had no good news to report to the old nun. The front doorbell rang and almost immediately afterward there was the sound of imperious knocking. Ringing and knocking went on almost nonstop until Joyce went to the door, and a moment later there was the distinctive sound of Richard rushing down the hall. He came to a stop in the doorway and looked triumphantly at Dunning.

"Counselor! Fancy meeting you here."

"Oh come on, Moriarity. I know you've got a tail on me. What took you so long?"

Richard stepped back into the hall and shouted, "In the basement first. There's an apartment down there."

He came into the study and looked for reactions to the instructions he had just given. Doubtless, he was recalling other occasions when that basement apartment had harbored the one he sought. Thank God, he did not know how recently Lydia Hopkins had been downstairs while he spoke to Emtee Dempsey in the study. He sat in a chair beside the desk so that he was facing Dunning.

"You don't look worried."

"What, me worry?" Dunning crossed his blue eyes and assumed a comic smile.

"If she isn't here, where is she?"

"Lieutenant, I hope you are not suggesting that I would conspire to obstruct justice. As an officer of the court, I have an obligation to carry out its legitimate orders. Presumably, you feel the same about yours."

"Lydia Hopkins is under indictment. If you know where she is, you should tell me."

"You're absolutely right."

"Where is she?"

"I do not know."

Richard glared at him, then turned to Emtee Dempsey, who had followed this exchange impassively. "How about you, Sister? Where is Lydia Hopkins?"

"Richard, I am not an officer of the court. Nor am I a policeman."

It was the opening of a lengthy and pointless conversation between Richard and Sister Mary Teresa and Kim wished her brother would not proceed from such a weak position. O'Connell and Gleason, Richard's assistants, came to report that the basement apartment was empty and received permission to look upstairs as well, although their expressions made it clear they thought they were on a wild goose chase and blamed Richard for it. Richard's problem was that he had come convinced he would find Lydia Hopkins in the house and was reluctant to let the idea go even after it had been disproved. All in all, it was a disastrous visit.

Until the telephone call.

And then it turned disastrous for the others in the study.

Emtee Dempsey handed the phone to Richard and he put it to his ear, clearly grateful for the distraction. Within moments, he straightened in his chair, then stood. It was clear from his expression that what he was hearing was important. Why was Kim already certain that it was relevant to what they had just been speaking of? Richard put down the phone and said to Kim.

"You talked with a Dolores Merrill this morning?"

"At lunch."

"What did she tell you?"

Emtee Dempsey interrupted, "Why are you asking, Richard?"

"Because her body has just been found. At the Elm Stand Club."

64

"Dead?"

Richard nodded but all Kim could think of was the intense, pretty woman who had sat across from her and played with a spoon as she spoke of being threatened by Lydia.

"Surely you are not accusing Sister Kimberly," Emtee Dempsey said.

Richard smiled unpleasantly, but it was Dunning he addressed.

"I think *you* know who *I* think did it."

"Be careful, Moriarity."

"You want to give her an alibi, tell me where she is."

Richard left, slamming the front door when he went out. Dunning got to his feet.

He said, "I wish now they had found her here."

Four

❖

The telephone call that brought news of the murder of Dolores Merrill to the house on Walton Street was bad enough. But the call from Joyce shortly after was worse, even though, at first, Kim didn't understand its significance.

"Can you hear?" Joyce asked, and Kim listened because it was obvious Joyce was holding the phone out so that the roar of Lake Michigan could come over the phone from their lake place in Indiana.

"Hear that?" Joyce cried, as if she were producing the sound by fiat. "It's the monster that's eating the shoreline."

"You're in Indiana," Kim said.

"Weren't you told?"

"It makes lying easier if I know less."

"You never told a lie in your life. Did Elsie get back?"

"Elsie?"

"You know," Joyce said significantly.

"Isn't she with you?"

"Well, she can't very well be in two places at once. Emtee Dempsey called and asked her to go back there. Leaving poor me without a car, stranded at the beach. I'm thawing out a steak, there's beer in the fridge. . . ."

"Joyce, she isn't here. Look, I'll talk to Emtee, then I'll call you back."

"But she called here," Joyce was saying as Kim returned the phone to its cradle. She was in the kitchen to fetch a gin and tonic for William Dunning when the phone rang. The door to the basement was closed. Kim crossed to it, let herself through to the kitchen stairway, and pulled the door shut behind her.

Going down the stairs to the basement apartment, she felt that she was invading Lydia's privacy, but that made no sense. Gleason and O'Connell had presumably searched the place high and low and found it empty. Was it possible that Lydia had been there and not been found? Or had come in since the search was made? Kim would have preferred telling Emtee Dempsey about Joyce's phone call first, but with William Dunning in the study that might be imprudent. The lawyer had come to the house only because he had been assured that Lydia was elsewhere. Before Joyce called, Kim had considered how fortunate it was, given Dolores Merrill's expression of fear that noon, that there could be no question where Lydia was when Dolores was killed. Where in the world was Lydia now?

The door of the apartment was ajar and meager light came from the ceiling light that had been left on by the police. Kim looked in. The living room had an unfriendly look, illumined from above rather than by the floor and table lamps. Kim's hand was on the switch when she had the odd feeling that she should leave things just as they were.

"Lydia?"

67

Her voice sounded timid, half frightened, and she called again, louder, but no less unnaturally, listening to her voice echo in the empty room. She crossed the room and passed into the little kitchenette off which a door led to the bedroom. This door too had been left open but there was no light within. Kim called Lydia's name again, a kind of warning, and reached inside the door, searching for the light switch. She found it and, having turned it on, looked inside. Empty. How tightly the bed was made, everything tucked in, the spread folded and placed on a chair in the corner of the room. Simple. Yet Lydia had remarked on how cluttered and comfortable the apartment was after prison. She had simplified the bedroom, at least. And there were bars on the windows.

Thoughts of prison, of why Lydia had been sent there, of the death that very day of Dolores Merrill, a woman with whom she herself had spoken in the dining room of the Elm Stand Country Club only a few hours ago, a woman who had professed to be filled with fear at the thought of Lydia Hopkins being free once more—such thoughts tumbled after one another in her mind and she realized that she had, during the course of the past few days, lost the ability to dismiss them.

There was a sound of tapping. Kim instinctively flicked off the light and stayed right where she was, alert, heart in her throat, waiting. The tapping began again. The window. Thank God she had turned off the light, but the light from behind her must silhouette her in the doorway. In a single movement, Kim backed out of the bedroom and pulled the door shut after her. It was while she was shutting the door that she saw the shadow at the window.

It stayed with her as an afterimage, which is why she did not immediately flee upstairs. The tapping was a signal, meant for her. Whoever was out there had seen her. Kim slowly opened the door again. She narrowed her eyes and could see someone crouched at the basement window. Who else would it be but Lydia?

But Lydia would know that there were bars over the window. In this neighborhood such precautions had to be taken. Kim put the folded spread on the bed, moved the chair under the window, and stood on it. She tried to turn the lock, but could not. She tapped back and then realized Lydia could no longer see her except as an indistinct shape. Kim got down from the chair, turned on the light and then pointed before leaving the room.

She went hurriedly through the apartment and up the stairs to the kitchen and the back door. She unlocked it and hardly had it open before Lydia pushed her way inside.

"Thank God you saw me."

"Where have you been?"

"Don't ask. I had trouble with the VW, it has taken me forever to get back."

"But why didn't you ring the bell?"

"Because I recognized Bill Dunning's car outside. What's going on? I was sent away so he could visit and then I'm summoned back and he's still here."

"Summoned back by whom?"

"By Sister Mary Teresa. Look at my hands." She displayed them, gritty and streaked with grease. "Changing the tire was bad enough but I had engine trouble on the Skyway and pulled off on Stony Island Boulevard just before it stopped for good. I'm going to take a shower." She turned to go downstairs, then stopped. "Thank you, Sister." Her hand was briefly on Kim's arm and then she was gone.

Kim hurriedly mixed William Dunning's gin and tonic and marched into the study with it. If there were explanations to be given, they must come from Sister Mary Teresa.

"Did you have to go out for something?" Emtee Dempsey asked.

"No."

There was an awkward silence. The old nun said, "Mr. Dunning went to see what had happened to you."

"And didn't find me? I went downstairs for a few minutes."

"Quite a few minutes. Who was on the telephone?"

"Joyce called."

"Is everything all right?"

"Just as you wanted it," Kim answered.

Mr. Dunning sipped his drink and followed the exchange as if it were a tennis match. If Emtee Dempsey caught the significance of Kim's answer, she gave no sign.

"Sister had a conversation with Mrs. Merrill earlier today," the old nun informed William Dunning. "At the country club."

"Poor Dolores," Dunning said, turning his drink as if it were a gyroscope.

"Why so?"

"She caused me real trouble at the trial, babbling about having been threatened by Lydia, pretending to have had an affair with Jeff. . . ."

"Pretending?"

"If Jeff Hopkins had been tempted to stray, he certainly wouldn't have been attracted by someone as neurotic as Dolores Merrill. Dolores is a compulsive golfer, a compulsive bridge player. Once she was a compulsive eater but she got over that, becoming almost anorectic in compensation. Her husband is a very able, very successful surgeon, which leaves Dolores with much time on her hands." He paused. "I can't speak of her in the past tense, I just can't. Don't get the wrong impression. She was a very sweet person. But she developed the crazy idea that Lydia meant to kill her."

"That's what she told me today," Kim said.

"I'm not at all surprised. She got over it, but Lydia's release brought it all back."

"And now she is dead," Emtee Dempsey said. "How I wish we had more details."

There was nothing on the evening news, of course, or almost nothing. Toward the end of the half hour of local news, there was a bulletin, but no details. Mrs. Dolores Merrill, Chicago society personality, had been found dead at home on the grounds of the Elm Stand Town & Country Club. Preliminary indications were that her death was not due to natural causes.

"Thank God Lydia can't be suspected. Tell me, Sister, where did you send her?"

The old nun smiled sweetly. "Don't you think we should keep that a secret still, Mr. Dunning."

"So long as I can rest assured that her alibi is airtight."

"Of that you can be perfectly certain," the old nun said and she directed her beaming face at Kim. Kim could not bear it. It was one thing for the old nun to mislead her sisters in religion, but it was something else to permit Mr. Dunning to believe that Lydia was far from the house and safe from any possible questions about where she had been during this afternoon and evening. Fortunately, Mr. Dunning had risen to his feet, his drink hardly touched.

"On that comforting note, I will say good-bye. It is a gruesome thought, but it does occur to me that Dolores Merrill's death will turn attention away from Lydia, at least for a time."

"Sister Kimberly will see you to the door, Mr. Dunning. Thank you so much for coming by."

What would the lawyer have thought if he were told

that Lydia was at this moment in the house, that what he had called her alibi would involve a story about changing a tire in Indiana and then the Volkswagen conking out on Stony Island Boulevard? All that put her a long way from the country club, but even so. . . .

When Kim closed the door after Mr. Dunning, she hurried back to the study. Emtee Dempsey sat with closed eyes, her small hands making a Christmas tree on the desk before her.

"She is back, Sister. I suppose you can tell yourself you didn't know that for certain when you reassured Mr. Dunning. I suppose you can explain it in all sorts of ways that satisfy your conscience, but I have never—"

"What are you saying?" Sister Mary Teresa looked at Kim with a startled expression on her face.

"I'm saying that Elsie returned in answer to your summons."

"My summons?" She made an impatient gesture with her hand. "Lydia Hopkins is in the house?"

"Yes."

"Please ask her to come here at once."

"She was about to take a shower."

"Then she can come from her shower. I want to see her immediately."

"Didn't you know?"

For answer, Kim received the most pained expression she had ever seen on the old nun's face.

"Please, Sister."

Bewildered, Kim went once more down the hall. Was it possible that Lydia had come back without being asked? But then . . . Kim brought her hands together in a slapping motion. No! She was sick to death of speculation about Lydia Hopkins. Let Sister Mary Teresa unravel this if she could. Sister Kimberly Moriarity no longer cared to form an opinion on the innocence or guilt of Lydia Hopkins.

Lydia wore a robe and had a towel wrapped around her head and a smile on her just-scrubbed face.

"Has he gone?"

Kim nodded. "Sister Mary Teresa wants to see you."

"That's why I'm here."

Observing the subsequent confrontation in the study, Kim found herself torn between doubt and belief. If Sister Mary Teresa's claim that she had not telephoned the house in Indiana and summoned Lydia back was sincere, did that mean Lydia was lying?

"You thought you were speaking to me?"

Lydia nodded her head slowly in assent. "But who else could it have been?"

"Sister has a distinctive voice," Kim said, but it was merely an observation. Even as she made it, she remembered what the phone at the lake house did to familiar voices.

Emtee Dempsey lifted her hands impatiently. "However it was done, it was done. Someone telephoned the beach house, impersonated me, and told you to return here. It was not I. Who could it be? A first condition is knowledge of your whereabouts. A very limited number of people knew you were staying here. No one other than Sister Joyce and myself knew you were going to be in Indiana. The explanation is simple. You were followed."

Kim said, "The follower would have had to know Lydia was here."

"Perhaps. But that knowledge need not have been had prior to their leaving." But she was frowning. "I don't like it."

She meant that she did not like simply to invent a

73

logically possible explanation. There were uncountable logically possible explanations.

"Did you use the telephone, apart from taking this mendacious call?"

"Mendacious," Lydia repeated. She took pleasure in the old nun's unusual vocabulary.

"The caller who claimed to be me?"

"No."

"Who answered the phone?" Kim asked.

"I did. Joyce was busy in the kitchen. Besides, you were the only one who knew we were there."

"Apparently not."

Joyce and Lydia alone in the house, the phone rings, only one person knows they are there, Lydia answers and, sure enough, it is Sister Mary Teresa, ordering her to return at once.

"What reason was given?"

"You said . . ." Lydia stopped and gave Emtee Dempsey an apologetic smile. "Sorry. The woman said that something had happened and it was important I come back at once."

"What time was this?"

"We hadn't been there an hour. Three o'clock?"

"Something was about to happen, something the caller must have known would happen."

"What?"

The news of the death of Dolores Merrill did not produce any particular reaction in Lydia. She listened, she thought about it.

"It happened this afternoon?"

"Yes. A wild question, Lydia. Could the voice on the phone have been Dolores Merrill's?"

"The voice was your voice, Sister, no one else's."

"Mr. Dunning spoke of your alibi. He took comfort from the fact that you were altogether elsewhere at the

74

time Dolores Merrill was killed. You will understand the reason for his relief. If you had been in this house at the time of the murder, suspicion could not possibly be directed at you. So too if you were across the border in Indiana. What we must do is reconstruct as exactly as we can your movements from the time you left Joyce."

But they must also fetch Joyce from the beach house in Indiana, her presence there no longer being necessary to mask the fact that Lydia Hopkins was also in the house. Kim of course was expected to make the round trip.

"If the car is ready, that is."

Lydia said, "He didn't think it was serious. A water pump, and he was sure he could put it in today."

"Where exactly is the place?"

"Sister, I'll go. I know where it is and it's my fault this happened."

"Not on your life, dear lady," Emtee Dempsey said. "It is more important than ever that you keep out of harm's way."

Lydia argued the point for five minutes but eventually gave Kim a greasy calling card bearing the legend GAL-VIN'S GARAGE and an address on Stony Island Boulevard.

"How will you get there?" Emtee Dempsey asked.

"A cab."

"Wouldn't it make far more sense to have Sister Joyce return from the lake by cab?"

"It would make more dollars than sense. I mean for the cabby. I'll get her."

Galvin's Garage was located on a corner; there were three black men in attendance, one who frowned, one who smiled and one with the impassive expression of the Buddha.

"Has it been repaired?" Kim asked.

The smiler had the name CHARLEY embroidered on his shirt. "What repairs?"

"I think you were going to put in a new water pump."

The three consulted on this. A sheaf of greasy forms was gone through by each in turn.

"No bill for any repairs here. You owe twelve dollars for parking."

"The car was left here because something was wrong with it. I was told it needed a new water pump."

"Who told you that?"

"The person who left it here was told that."

The smile faltered, then firmed. "This isn't your car?"

"It's our car."

"Someone told your husband that car needed a water pump?"

Why was she pursuing this idiotic conversation? It would have been far more sensible to just pay the twelve dollars and drive to Indiana and pick up Joyce. But Kim had become stubborn.

"The car belongs to my religious community. I am a nun. Sister Kimberly Moriarity."

"You're a nun?" Charley's smile widened, exposing more teeth. "A Ro-man Cath-o-lic nun?"

"That's right."

"Who was here when the car was left?" He squinted at her slyly.

"I don't know." Kim showed Charley the calling card. "She was given this."

Charley laughed aloud. "Why, Patrick Galvin gave her that. He's the only one who gives out that card. I am Ro-man Catholic too!"

Kim smiled, paused a minute, then said, "Could you check the car carefully to make sure it doesn't need a water pump?"

"Sister, if Patrick thought you needed a water pump, he

would have filled out one of these." He flourished the sheaf of forms. "These are job orders. There is no job order for that VW."

"Where is Mr. Galvin now?"

"Home."

"Maybe if you called him . . ."

"On his day off? Uh-uh. Do you have any holy cards?"

No direction this conversation took could surprise Kim now.

"Why?"

"I want to pin it up back here and tell Patrick that a Roman Catholic nun was here and made this place holy and it will drive him crazy?"

"Why?"

"He hates Catholics, that's why." Charley delivered this as if it were a punch line.

"Is he Protestant?"

"Not anymore. He had a conversion. Now he's a muslin."

"Muslim."

"Yeah. He's going to change his name and be Muhammad something or other and good-bye Galvin."

Once Kim's father had met a black bearing the name O'Neil and never got over it. What would he have made of a black Patrick Galvin who hated Catholics and was now a convert to Islam? "Can you check the car and make sure it's safe to drive?"

The VW was driven inside, put on a lift, and raised high enough for the frowning and Buddha-like blacks to examine it thoroughly. Wires were attached and gauges read. The car was let down and the examination continued.

Charley asked again about holy cards and Kim told him she did not have any.

"You got anything that will prove you're a nun and you've been here?"

Kim shook her head. She found Charley's intended use of whatever he had in mind dubious at best.

"I'll pray for him," she said.

"Oh, that's gooood. I tell him that he like to have a fit. I'll tell him you went all around this place laying blessings on everything."

The examination took forty-five minutes and there was nothing wrong with the car.

Charley told her he belonged to Holy Angels parish. "You know Father Clements?"

"I've heard about him."

"It's all true! I been trying to get him down here to talk to Patrick but he's just too busy and Patrick ain't going to go see no priest."

The examination and the parking came to fifteen dollars.

"Is that all?"

"You *want* trouble?"

"Inspecting the car is only three dollars?"

"Consider it a gift from Muhammad Galvin."

"Is the spare tire all right?"

"The spare tire is fine."

"It should be flat."

"Why you want a flat spare tire?"

On the drive to Indiana Kim pondered the significance of Lydia's lying about the car. Perhaps that was too strong. She had said that after she changed the tire, the car began to make odd noises, which was believable enough, and that she had cut the speed to practically nothing, creeping along for miles until she pulled off at Stony Island and into the first filling station she came to. And she had been so definite about the water pump. Some part that had to be replaced. That is why she left the car. But she had been definite about the flat tire too.

Fifteen minutes after Kim arrived at the beach house, Richard burst through the door followed by an overweight deputy sheriff with a search warrant. The sheriff went upstairs but Richard stood in the double doorway looking out at the deck where Joyce and Kim were drinking coffee from mugs shaped like Teddy bears.

"We're searching the house."

"Looking for anything in particular?"

"The same thing I was looking for at Walton Street."

"She's not here either."

Richard turned and went inside, giving Kim the chance she had not taken at once to ask Joyce about the phone call that had brought Lydia back to town the day before.

"Who answered the phone?"

"I was outside. Lydia was hanging up as I came in."

"Did you hear the phone ring?"

Joyce frowned. "Why?"

"Did you hear her talking?"

Joyce looked closely at Kim while she thought about it. "She was talking when I came in, then hung up. At first, I thought she didn't want me to see that she had been on the phone. But then she turned and told me it had been Emtee Dempsey."

Although the surface of her mug was cool from the chill air coming off the lake, the coffee itself was still hot. On the metallic surface of the lake, a ship low in the water seemed at anchor, but ten minutes before it had not been there.

What if no one had telephoned and Lydia only pretended to be ending a conversation with Emtee Dempsey when Joyce came in? One thing was certain. It was just as

79

easy to pretend to get a phone call as to pretend it was from Emtee Dempsey. It gave Lydia an excuse to leave the house. More than four hours later, she showed up on Walton Street. The reason she gave for taking so long on a trip that normally took one hour was car trouble. But there had been no car trouble. Maybe Galvin would remember when the car was left there, maybe he wouldn't. It could have been forty minutes after she left the beach. That gave her hours of unaccounted-for time. A period during which Dolores Merrill, who professed to be terrified by the thought that Lydia Hopkins was running around free, had been killed.

Lydia had lied to Sister Mary Teresa about the car, so forget the phone call. The conclusion was inescapable. Someone Emtee Dempsey was attempting to help was deceiving her. The car made Kim inclined to think the phone call was a hoax, too, and that it had provided Lydia with a chance to return to Chicago. Why?

From inside the house came the sound of male voices, one obviously angry. The front door slammed and Richard joined them.

"Got any more of that coffee?"

"Find anything?"

Richard glared out at the lake. The ship had moved eastward. Joyce got up and went for coffee.

"Did you follow me from the house?"

"You were followed," he said, somewhat smugly, but she could tell he was not happy to have come all this way for nothing.

Joyce came back with coffee for Richard. "Did I miss anything?"

Richard took the coffee but ignored the questions. "How long you staying here, Kim?"

"We're going right back."

He thought about it. "You came here to pick up Joyce?"

"That's right."

"How long you been here, Sister?"

"I came out yesterday."

A sea gull suspended motionlessly above the deck cawed. Richard, having tasted his coffee, looked strangely at Joyce.

"How did you get here?"

Kim's grip on her coffee mug tightened. Good Lord, of course. If Joyce drove here yesterday, how did the car get back to Chicago? Kim felt a small pride at Richard's astuteness but it fled before her recognition that he had caught them.

"I'm insulted," Joyce said.

"Why?"

"Obviously you didn't follow *me* when I left Walton Street."

"How did you get here?"

Joyce tossed her head. "I don't suppose you ever heard of buses."

Kim managed not to sigh with relief. Richard stood and drained his coffee. "Well, I won't offer you a ride. Get the car fixed up?"

"It runs like a watch."

They waited for the door to close. "It wasn't a lie," Joyce said.

"No."

"Do you think it was?"

"You asked him a question."

"But it was meant to make him think I took a bus out here. I'll have to confess it. Do you think he will check the buses?"

What was Joyce's fear, that she had told a lie or that Richard would catch her in it? All Kim knew was that she was glad Joyce had said what she did. She herself had been convinced that Richard's question was their Waterloo.

81

On the trip back to Chicago, Kim drove and listened to
Joyce talk about a trade the Cubs had made the day before,
one she was sure was not to the advantage of the North
Side team. Joyce did not expect Kim to answer, and the
truth was Kim hadn't the least idea what Joyce was talking
about, so it was a perfect conversation, leaving Kim free to
ponder what she had learned and what and how she
should tell Emtee Dempsey. She could not let Lydia go on
making a fool of the old nun.

Lydia was in the study and that was good. Good too that
Emtee Dempsey got them right onto the topic Kim wanted
to discuss.

"Well, you're back. Now much was the car?"

Lydia said, "I'll pay the bill."

"Nothing was wrong with the car. I had to pay only a
parking fee."

Silence fell, during which Emtee Dempsey looked with
lifted brows at Lydia, who lowered her head. After a minute, she lifted her eyes and looked at the old nun.

"Sister Mary Teresa, I misled you. I came to town yesterday in response to an urgent request. I left the car at the
garage on Stony Island with the intention of going back for
it when I was done. I lied to you twice."

"Why?"

Lydia drew her lower lip between her teeth. "I won't lie
to you again."

"I am glad to hear that."

"But I can't tell you why I came to town."

Sister Mary Teresa smiled benevolently at Lydia. "You
came back in response to a phone call?"

"I can't tell you who I came to see."

"Lydia, whoever brought you back to town effectively
destroyed your alibi when Dolores Merrill was killed. It is
conceivable that you were brought just for that reason.

Unless I know who you came to see, I cannot know that. You did see the person in question?"

"Sister, I would rather not say anything more. I just can't tell you who it was."

"You have no obligation to do that, of course."

"If you want me to leave, I will."

"As a postulant, you are under obedience to me, Sister. I will not invoke that fact and ask you again who you came to see yesterday. But I will certainly not give you permission to leave the house."

Kim was surprised by her own self-control. That Emtee Dempsey should continue the fiction that Lydia Hopkins's stay in the house was a probationary period before entering the Order of Martha and Mary was preposterous. The fact that Lydia said she was sorry for telling at least two blatant lies to Sister Mary Teresa did not, in Kim's mind, diminish her guilt. Particularly when she refused to give a true account of her movements the previous day. The woman had accepted their hospitality, benefiting from Sister Mary Teresa's assumption of her innocence of the grisly murders of her husband and daughter. She had left Joyce alone in Indiana, abandoned the VW in a garage miles from Walton Street, then gone to talk with some mysterious person. By this time, Kim had stopped believing anything Lydia said. Her anger was not based on the fact that Lydia's deception had sent her on a wild goose chase that took up a good part of her day, but of course that did add to it. She was further angered by Emtee Dempsey's bland acceptance of this situation.

"Lydia, let us drop the subject for now. I will ask you to reconsider keeping secret the name of the person who summoned you."

"You are very patient with me."

"I am taking into account the fact that you have been

through years of anguish which seem not to have reached their end."

That was a statement borne out decisively when Kim and Emtee Dempsey sat before the television on the sun porch later watching the evening news. Judge Franklin Boone had issued a warrant for the arrest of Lydia Hopkins in response to the prosecutor's request.

That Lydia would be tried again for the murder of her husband and daughter was now a certainty.

Five

W hen Richard described for Kim and Joyce the circumstances of Dolores Merrill's death, Joyce said, *"Sunset Boulevard."*

"What are you talking about?"

"The movie," Kim said. "Forget it."

The body of Dolores Merrill had been found floating facedown, just like William Holden's in the film. What they did not know was how she had gotten there.

"Oh, she didn't just fall in. That is certain. She had been clobbered from behind with a poolside table."

"How large a table?" Emtee Dempsey asked. Lydia had been hurried into the chapel when Richard appeared on the front porch, and presumably now knelt veiled and praying on a prie-dieu. Richard had never checked the chapel when searching the house before, and they were counting on that now, but if Emtee Dempsey felt any unease she did not show it.

Richard described the table—light, small, aluminum. "Not enough to knock her out, if that's what you mean."

"How did she die?"

"Drowning."

"That is the complete explanation?"

"No. Did you ever see a pool skimmer?"

"Tell me about it."

The theory the police had developed involved the long-handled skimmer that had been put to a grisly use. Marks on the back of Dolores's neck suggested that she had been held underwater. The drenched organdy dress twisted around the body bore testimony to the violence of the struggle in which Dolores Merrill had lost her grip on life.

"Pushed in, then held underwater?"

"That's right. I pulled Bill Dunning in as a material witness but he refused to say a word."

"A material witness to what?"

"He is Lydia Hopkins's lawyer. There is no way confidentiality between lawyer and client can cover harboring a fugitive."

"Why is that? If she told him where she was wouldn't she have told him that in confidence?"

"Ask Rush to explain it to you," Richard advised. He frowned. "We couldn't keep him forever, of course. He spoke when he got outside. Claims he'll sue for false arrest."

"I fail to see why his being Lydia's lawyer makes him a material witness to anything having to do with the unfortunate death of Mrs. Merrill."

"You don't, huh?"

"No, I don't. That's why I'm asking."

"Think about it."

"It's thinking about it that made me ask."

"You tell her, Kim. I'm going."

86

"He means they think Lydia killed Dolores." Kim took a bitter pleasure in telling Emtee Dempsey this.

"What nonsense." Emtee Dempsey rose and headed their little procession to the chapel for evening prayers. Kim wanted to get in front of the old nun and stop her, make her see that she was making a fool of herself by flying in the face of the facts about Lydia. But Joyce, as if sensing Kim's impatience, took her arm and shook her head. Kim held her tongue. Of course Joyce was right. Anything she said would be overheard by Lydia in the chapel.

But the chapel was empty.

Joyce looked as surprised as Kim, but Emtee Dempsey went to her place and knelt. Was it possible that she had not noticed Lydia was not here? Kim bent down and whispered in the old nun's ear, "Lydia isn't here."

The great starched headdress nodded and that was all. Emtee Dempsey knew and was unsurprised. Kim went to her place and knelt and tried to bring herself consciously into the presence of God but she was so irritated by Emtee Dempsey's whole attitude toward Lydia that her mind was a booming, buzzing confusion of distracting thoughts. She joined in their common recitation of the Divine Office, but her mind was anywhere but in the chapel. It did not help to tell herself that Emtee Dempsey assumed Lydia had gone downstairs and that was all there was to it. But Emtee Dempsey would have wanted Lydia to be with them in chapel as they ended their day in prayers. After all, the fiction was that Lydia was preparing herself for reception into the Order of Martha and Mary, the M&M's, the improbable first step toward the reconstitution of a once-thriving order that was now reduced to its three remaining members in the house on Walton Street.

Lydia should be with them in chapel, saying her prayers, asking forgiveness for the lies she had told.

As they recited the Psalms, Kim was further irritated by the clear, untroubled tone of Emtee Dempsey's voice. Of course, the old nun could quickly shut off the world, sink swiftly and deeply into a meditative trance, no matter how occupied she might be. At other times, Kim had been impressed, even edified, by this capacity to put the world so completely out of mind, but tonight it seemed deranged.

There, she had thought it explicitly. Sooner or later, the old nun's mind must go. She was in excellent health, no matter her short and pudgy self, and her memory still delivered up on demand thousands of unrelated facts on each of which she could train her analytic mind. There had been no sign of diminution in her mental faculties. Or had there? This fixation on Lydia's innocence, despite the past findings and present complications, could be the first sign that the old nun was finally losing her grip. It had to happen sometime, so why not now? The difficulty with this hypothesis was that it could scarcely be verified without alerting the old nun to what she was doing. She would have to settle for a less rigorous test. Besides, she was no psychiatrist. What exactly did she mean by "losing her mind"?

Kim could imagine repartee with Emtee Dempsey on such a question, with the old nun sure to trot out a ready-made but generally authentic definition. Better that than to go ga-ga, opening herself to public derision when the police found Lydia guilty of her husband's and daughter's deaths and most likely responsible for the death of Dolores as well.

As long as she could not pray, Kim decided to sketch out in her mind the case against Lydia Hopkins.

Had she learned anything whatsoever that lent support to Emtee Dempsey's conviction that Lydia was innocent?

Kim's visit to the country club and her talk with Lydia's neighbors made it necessary for Lydia to have undergone a profound transformation of personality during her years in prison. Those who had known her before found it entirely plausible that Lydia had committed two unnatural murders. One person, Dolores Merrill, now dead, had professed to be terrified at the thought that Lydia Hopkins was free, a fear that was justified, whether or not the object of the fear was well grounded. Things would be simple if Lydia had been in the house on the lake with Joyce when Dolores was killed. Hadn't Bill Dunning made the point, when the news of Dolores's death came, that Lydia had an alibi? And Emtee Dempsey had assured the lawyer that Lydia could not possibly come under suspicion for this new murder. Minutes later, Lydia tapped on the basement window and came in with the story that a phone call from Emtee Dempsey had brought her back to town. Had there even been a phone call? If that was not a lie, nonetheless the story of the car's breakdown had itself broken down. Lydia's almost blithe admission that she had lied was received with aplomb by Emtee Dempsey, who was also unfazed to find that Lydia was no longer in the chapel. Kim realized that it was the old nun who really puzzled her.

Emtee Dempsey was seated now, head tipped forward, her great starched headdress immobile. A stranger might have thought her asleep, but Kim knew better. The old nun was a woman of deep spirituality and maturity, whose mind put her in the front rank of intellectuals. Her reputation as an historian was worldwide, but if she moved with ease through the past, she had great insight into the present. She was no woolgathering, absentminded professor. Far from it. Her ability to read the motives of actors in events of which she could not have had any firsthand experience was uncanny. With a sureness she was infuriated to have called intuition she could identify the perpetrator of a crime she knew of only through what others told her. She had never been wrong in assessments of guilt or innocence, which never ceased to impress Kim. Kim had doubted the old nun in the past only to find that it was she, not Emtee Dempsey, who was mistaken.

All that was true, but Kim now had the sickening certainty that Sister Mary Teresa was dead wrong to think that Lydia Hopkins was innocent.

Kim was also sure that her own and Joyce's skepticism combined would not deflect Sister Mary Teresa from the path she was on. She had vowed to prove Lydia innocent and she would never go back on that promise.

Not that Kim meant to sit by and watch her model and heroine make an utter fool of herself. But what to do?

Joyce offered to check the basement apartment before they all went upstairs to bed. Emtee Dempsey shook her head.

"I told Lydia to move upstairs with us. It seemed inhospitable to keep her down there in the basement."

It was all Kim could do not to exchange a look of disbelief with Joyce.

"What room?" Joyce asked.

"The one next to mine."

"Right or left?"

Had Joyce lost her mind too? What difference did it make which room Lydia was in? Now they were all involved in the charade that the woman was a postulant. Kim pulled the door of her own room shut behind her with unnecessary firmness and stood with clenched fists, wondering if she were only being childish to react so negatively to a deed that could be construed as one of charity and compassion. Maybe if there were only the past murders to worry about she could have brought it off, but the image of Dolores Merrill floating facedown in her pool

90

made it impossible. Kim decided she must do something to turn Sister Mary Teresa from the course she was on.

When Mr. Timothy Rush, their silver-haired lawyer, showed up on the doorstep the following morning just as they were returning from the cathedral, Kim thought it was providential.

"Have breakfast with us, Timothy," Sister Mary Teresa said. Her voice suggested that she was relieved to have someone her own age to talk with. Kim prayed that Emtee Dempsey meant to consult the lawyer about Lydia. That would mean the old nun was not as far gone as she seemed. Surely, if anyone would react with alarm to what they were doing, that person was Timothy Rush. He might on occasion be a reluctant collaborator when the old nun was sailing close to the wind, but he could never condone harboring a fugitive from justice.

"You haven't met Sister Elsie," the old nun said, indicating the bundled-up figure of Lydia, who was coming from the car with Joyce. The old nun leaned toward the lawyer. "A postulant at last."

Mr. Rush smiled and nodded and went inside with Emtee Dempsey and that, until breakfast, was that.

Neither Lydia nor Joyce sat at table with Sister Mary Teresa, Mr. Rush, and Kim. Joyce of course was cooking; Lydia waited on them, slipping dishes onto the table, then taking up a post demurely behind Mr. Rush when she wasn't in the kitchen with Joyce. Perhaps Mr. Rush took this for virginal modesty or obedience; whatever, he paid no attention to Lydia and she certainly was not the topic of conversation. So far as talk at the breakfast table went, it would seem that Emtee Dempsey had summoned the lawyer to Walton Street in order to talk about the novels of Thomas Hardy she was presently rereading. From time to time, Mr. Rush got in a word about William Dean Howells, observing that the American contemporary of Hardy was a favorite of his, but Emtee Dempsey had begun a disquisition on *The Return of the Native* and Mr. Rush was fated to hear it all. Eventually the two elderly people adjourned to the study. Kim waited to see if her presence would be required, but it was not.

As the door of the study closed, Emtee Dempsey was saying, "And now, Timothy, I have a very serious matter to discuss with you."

Kim could have cheered. She pushed through into the kitchen. Joyce stood in the half-open outside door smoking a cigarette furtively. She had already pitched it outside before she saw it was Kim.

"Good heavens, don't scare me like that." The words emerged like smoke signals. "I ought to retrieve it."

"Light another."

"Are you giving me permission?"

"If you want to call it that. Where's you-know-who?"

"In her room."

"Upstairs?"

"We wouldn't want to be inhospitable."

"Joyce, I think our problem is solved. Emtee is talking with Mr. Rush about a very serious matter. Her words."

"That could mean anything."

Kim skipped up to her room. Lydia's door was closed and Kim felt bad about feeling so good that Lydia would soon be leaving. Leaving to be arrested and tried for one murder and retried for two others. Her destination was prison, probably for the rest of her life, certainly for most of it. How could Kim rejoice at that prospect? In the circumstances it was really not surprising that Lydia should lie and act oddly. Who wouldn't?

But as true as all that was, Kim's first loyalty was to Sister Mary Teresa, who was now flouting the law and running the risk of public ridicule because of her proclaimed intention of proving Lydia Hopkins was innocent.

There was one great flaw in that project. Lydia was guilty. When that was proved, Sister Mary Teresa's reason for harboring the fugitive would open her to wounding and deflating criticism.

Kim realized she no longer doubted Lydia's guilt. No amount of compassion could alter it, nor was it their job to substitute their feelings of sympathy for justice. After all, they did not have the power to forgive Lydia for what she had done.

Kim sat in a chair by the window, waiting to be summoned downstairs. She tried to read, but could not concentrate. In such circumstances, Emtee Dempsey would have meditated or said the Rosary. She certainly would not have sat like a lump looking out at the traffic going by on Walton Street.

Fifteen minutes passed, then a half hour, and Kim's phone had not rung. She opened the door of her room and looked out. The door across the hall was still closed. Kim went to the stairs and on down to the kitchen. Everything had been restored to spic-and-span order and Joyce sat at the table reading the sports page of the *Tribune*.

"Well, it didn't take long," she said, not looking up.

"What do you mean?"

"Mr. Rush left minutes after you went upstairs."

"He did! Why didn't you tell me?"

Joyce looked genuinely surprised. "Was I supposed to?"

"No. Oh, I'm sorry." Kim went rapidly down the hall to the study. The door was open. Emtee Dempsey was at her desk, bent over, writing slowly but steadily with a very large fountain pen, adding to the massive history of the twelfth century that had been her scholarly project for nearly five years. A day like any other. "Mr. Rush left?"

"That's right."

Kim pulled the door shut. "Did you talk with him about Lydia?"

"Not at length, Sister Kimberly. He has set in motion inquiries that will prove helpful if another trial takes place. Merely a precaution. I have every confidence that there will be no trial."

"Even after yesterday?"

"Yesterday?"

"Sister, she lied to you. Don't you see, when you assured Mr. Dunning that no suspicion could fall on Lydia you thought she was at the lake. She wasn't at the lake. For hours she was running around Chicago doing God knows what."

"Not only God, Sister. Lydia has explained all that to me."

"Has she? And what was the explanation?"

Emtee Dempsey frowned. "Perhaps it would be better if you didn't know."

"I'd like to know. I think Joyce and I have a right to know. Sister, there is a warrant for her arrest!"

"Issued by Judge Boone." The old nun's tone suggested that she knew a suspect warrant when she met one.

"She won't be rescued by Judge Marsh a second time."

"You spoke of a right to know."

"You've turned us into co-conspirators."

"I see, I see. Yes, you are right. Very well, there is only one solution."

"Sister, I don't like it any better than you do."

"Nonsense, you deserve a vacation."

"A vacation!"

"You and Joyce must go to the beach house. The change will do you good."

"You want *us* to leave?"

"I won't say that it did not occur to me that Sister Elsie's presence in the house involved us all in a common effort."

94

"Sister Elsie will be tried for murder. For three murders."

"I assure you she will not."

"On what basis?"

"Sister, I have not lived this long without acquiring some knowledge of the human heart. If I thought Lydia was guilty of any of those terrible deaths, I would act very differently than I am. I assure you of that."

Kim slumped into the chair across the desk from the old nun. "Can you give me one reason other than your ability to read the human heart why you think Lydia is innocent?"

"Of course."

"What is it?"

"She says she is and I believe her."

"That's not good enough."

"It is for me."

A chilly silence established itself, during which a dozen imaginary conversations boiled through Kim's mind. Finally, she stood and looked with exaggerated calm at Emtee Dempsey.

"We will not go to the lake. We will stay here and risk criminal charges along with you. Very likely the entire Order of Martha and Mary will end up in jail along with our new postulant."

Sister Mary Teresa laughed. "Of that you need have no fear."

Kim was not calm when she left the study. What an infuriating person the old nun could be. It was simply perverse to insist on Lydia's innocence when every sign pointed in the opposite direction. Emtee Dempsey was a champion of reason and a foe of intuition. She prided herself on being guided by the way things are rather than the way she might want them to be. But what hurt the most was that she had been willing to send Joyce and Kim to

Indiana and remain alone on Walton Street with Lydia Hopkins.

As she stalked down the hall, Kim thought of going directly to Mr. Rush and letting him know that Sister Mary Teresa had not told him everything about Lydia Hopkins. But then she had a far better idea. She would go to Katherine Senski.

Katherine was at home, not at the office in the *Tribune* building she still retained. Kim walked the few blocks to the North Shore building where Katherine lived, rose in the silent elevator to the fourteenth floor, and soon was seated contentedly, sipping tea but not particularly enjoying the stupendous view of Lake Michigan from Katherine's picture window. On the way over, she had rehearsed what she would say to this old friend and ally of Emtee Dempsey to make her see that the old nun was embarked on a course that would lead to disgrace and worse. Katherine needed little persuading.

"I couldn't agree more. It is completely and utterly mad. And," she added, fixing Kim with a stern and birdlike gaze, "very much like a dozen other escapades when she has made monkeys of the rest of us. Why should we think this time is different?"

"Because it is. Lydia Hopkins was found guilty after a long trial; she was freed on a technicality. There is now a warrant for her arrest on suspicion of murdering Dolores Merrill. I talked with Dolores; I know she was frightened to death of Lydia."

"But I understood that Lydia was safely in Indiana at the time."

"That is where she was supposed to be. She claims someone impersonating Sister telephoned to summon her back to Walton Street. But she lied to Emtee Dempsey about that. She parked the car at a garage over on Stony

Island, telling us it had developed engine trouble. That was a lie. For more than three hours she was somewhere in Chicago."

"And you think Elmhurst?"

"Katherine, I don't want to accuse her of something so awful, but what else can I think? There are many reasons to think her guilty and none that I know of to think her innocent."

Katherine wore a billowing, flowery, floor-length muumuu and began now to pace her modernistic living room. The furniture, the luxurious austerity, did not appeal to Sister Mary Teresa. Why did Kim think the two older women so much alike when they were so different? Katherine lit a cigarlike cigarette, and squinted thoughtfully into the smoke.

"If Sister Mary Teresa did not call her, who did?"

"She won't say. And Sister accepts her unwillingness to tell as if it were the most natural thing in the world. For all we know, there was no phone call. Maybe Lydia was the one who made a call."

"That could be checked easily enough. Finding out if someone called the lake place may not be so easy."

"How can I find out?"

"From the lake, it would have been a long-distance call. What company's long-distance service do you use from Indiana?"

Kim had got to her feet. Why hadn't she thought of that? Thank God, Katherine had.

"Why are you standing?"

"I'm going to check the calls from the lake. What a great idea."

"You don't have to run away to do that."

Predictably Katherine knew someone who could get this information for her. "She is with the Chicago police," Katherine added. "We wouldn't want to know anything the police don't know. Not that we'll mention why we're asking."

A call had been made.

One.

But it was Joyce's call because the call had been to the house on Walton Street. No other long-distance calls at all had been made from the beach house in Indiana during the billing period Katherine's informant checked, and that included every call recorded until sundown the previous day.

Except for Joyce's call, no other long-distance call had been made from or to the lake place. There was no doubt about it. An impersonal computer recorded in its circuitry the doings of the human clients of the telephone company, and to doubt its data was impossible.

"So she did lie," Kim said, and she could not keep a note of satisfaction from her voice.

"You already knew that. The question is why."

"In order to come back to town without Joyce and . . ." After a pause, Kim continued in an almost whisper, "To see Dolores Merrill."

"Sister Kimberly, you must put this before Sister Mary Teresa as clearly and forcibly as you can."

"Katherine, I have! Again and again. She simply refuses to consider seriously the possibility that Lydia is guilty of anything at all. And today she told me that she knows what Lydia was up to during the crucial hours because Lydia told her. Lydia!"

Katherine was pacing again, and when she turned her full dress wrapped around her like a flag, then freed itself to billow out once more. Her eyes were on some object in her mind, not in the room.

"I will speak to her, Sister."

"Good! I hoped you would."

"She is being duped, that seems clear." She looked

98

sternly at Kim. "But it is a solitary lapse, do you understand? Something that could happen to anyone. I will not have it attributed to her age."

Kim agreed, but she shared the dread Katherine's words were meant to exorcise. Was this indeed the beginning of Sister Mary Teresa's decline? Saddening as that prospect seemed to her, it carried for Katherine Senski a more personal relevance. After all, she and Emtee Dempsey were the same age.

Sister Mary Teresa sat quietly behind her desk, palms down on its surface, looking quizzically at Katherine as she laid out the case Kim had been making for several days. However understandable her sympathy for Lydia Hopkins, however attractive the prospect of showing that it was not just the fluke of a legal technicality that had returned Lydia to the ranks of the innocent, there were undeniably cogent reasons for doubting that innocence. Forget the fact that a jury trial of long duration and more than ordinary thoroughness had produced a guilty verdict. Forget the history of antic decisions by Judge Marsha Hunter.

"Judges! It is rather difficult to forget the warrant issued two days ago," the old nun murmured.

"Sister, it is not like you to concentrate on the accidental rather than the essential."

"And what is the essential?"

"I am reviewing it as dispassionately as I can. Let us go to the heart of the matter. Where was Lydia when Dolores Merrill was murdered in her swimming pool?"

"I have no idea."

"We can establish where she was not. She was not in this house. She was not at your house in Indiana. She parked your automobile, on the pretense of mechanical trouble, at a Chicago garage. That left her some three hours to wander around Chicago. More than enough time to go to Elmhurst."

Emtee Dempsey sat forward, receptive, as if anxious to follow what Katherine was saying. "How do you arrive at the three hours?"

"At least three hours," Kim broke in. "From the beach house to Stony Island Boulevard takes forty-five minutes at the most."

"In a well-running car. Yes, I see that. Have you made certain of the time the car was left at the garage?

"What on earth difference does that make, Sister Mary Teresa?" Katherine said. "The point is, the woman's whereabouts are unaccounted for during the crucial hours when Dolores Merrill was killed."

"Then you don't know when the car was left at the garage?"

"Perhaps Lydia told you when she left the car." There was an unaccustomed touch of sarcasm in Katherine's voice.

"She told all of us. The car developed alarming symptoms and she crept along the Skyway until she could turn off at Stony Island. If we compute the time she took to drive from the house in Indiana to the garage on the basis of, say, twenty-five miles an hour, perhaps even less, rather than fifty-five, then the amount of time you mentioned dwindles considerably."

"There was nothing wrong with the car," Kim said.

"In the event, no. But isn't it possible that, unused to our much-used little car, she *thought* it had developed trouble and quite sensibly slowed down and looked for a place to turn off? Sister Kimberly, nothing you learned at the Galvin Garage rules that out."

Katherine brought her hands together with a mild clapping sound. "Sister, please. Let me be blunt. Lydia has no alibi. There is a warrant for her arrest. Surely that was

100

neither sought nor issued without sufficient reasons having nothing to do with our ability to establish the exact time when Lydia dropped off your car at that garage."

"Has Richard told you something, Sister Kimberly?"

"If he had, I would have told you."

"I did not mean to suggest you would not."

Katherine's joined hands gave her the look of one at prayer. "Sister, will you concede that things look very bleak for Lydia Hopkins?"

"Indeed they do."

"Good. Then we are agreed that there are reasons not to think her innocent. What reasons are there for thinking she *is* innocent?"

Kim tensed, expecting Emtee Dempsey to invoke Lydia's word and her own willingness to accept it. But that was not the response.

"Lydia would be able to produce an alibi if it ever comes to that."

"Someone who can vouch for where she was?"

Emtee Dempsey nodded.

"Other than yourself?" Katherine asked after peering suspiciously at her old friend.

"Other than myself," Sister Mary Teresa said with a laugh.

"Have you talked with this person?" Katherine asked.

"No, I haven't."

Katherine's hands flew up and she sat back in her chair. "So we have come full circle. You accept this alibi on Lydia's say-so?"

Emtee Dempsey nodded gravely. "Yes, I do."

The interview came to an unsatisfactory ending, with both Katherine and Kim further convinced that Sister Mary Teresa was being willingly led down the garden path by

Lydia Hopkins. Kim accompanied Katherine to the front door and went out onto the porch to say good-bye.

"I have often admired her stubbornness in the past, Sister Kimberley. There have been times when it infuriated me. Never in the past has she been proved wrong and I right when this occurred. May this be another happy instance."

But Katherine did not look as if she thought it was. "She isn't making sense," Kim said sadly.

She offered to accompany the journalist home but Katherine shook her head, threw back her shoulders, and prepared to face the world. "I hope and pray we will be proved wrong and Sister Mary Teresa right."

Thus it was that it came as an answered prayer when, later that day, Adam Fenwick came forward to say that he had seen Lydia Hopkins during the crucial time when Dolores Merrill was killed.

Six

❖

Having returned to the house on Walton Street
with Katherine and having talked with Sister
Mary Teresa in the study, Kim went to Lydia's
room and knocked, determined to do something to extri-
cate Sister Mary Teresa from this impossible situation.
After a moment's silence, a remote voice asked her to
come in. Kim opened the door.

Lydia sat erectly in a chair by the window, hands grip-
ping its arms, her back pressed against the back of the
chair, her feet brought together and flat on the floor. Kim
had the unwelcome thought that Lydia was practicing
being executed. Lydia's eyes remained shut.

"I can come back," Kim said.

Lydia opened her eyes and looked at her. "No, come in.
What's the point of waiting? I know you must want to talk
to me."

Kim shut the door and sat on the bed. "You're right.
Lydia, I do feel sympathy with you. To the degree I can,

anyway. I haven't any idea what it is like to go through what you're going through."

"I deserve it."

Kim looked at her. Was this to be a confession? Lydia went on. "Most people deserve what they get, even if they are innocent of the specific thing they're accused of."

Kim nodded, somewhat deflated. "I suppose you're right." She steeled herself. "But I don't think Sister Mary Teresa deserves what you are doing to her."

Lydia nodded. "I know." Her eyes met Kim's. "Yesterday I didn't intend to come back. Even if I am proved innocent this time, the publicity will be bad for all of you. If I am meant to become one of you, there will be time for that after the trial. I didn't dream there would be another trial when I came here. I just wanted anonymity, to stop being someone watched and talked about."

"Why *did* you come back?" She could imagine Katherine applauding the question, but it had cost her much to ask it. Besides, she could not rid herself of the thought that Lydia had rehearsed this tack in order to disarm criticism.

"I was persuaded it was the only thing I could do."

"Persuaded by whom?"

Lydia turned and looked out the window. "It doesn't matter. The responsibility for returning is mine."

"How were you persuaded your return would not harm Sister Mary Teresa?"

A small Gioconda smile formed on Lydia's lips, then faded. "I'm afraid my own well-being was the major concern."

"Lydia, you must see that Sister is just blindly believing that everything will turn out all right. She has told people she will prove you're innocent. Do you know any reason for such confidence?"

"All I know is that her faith in me kept me going during some very dark days. It's hard to describe what it is like when no one believes you, when everybody thinks you have done dreadful things. Even former friends think so. Then I heard from Sister Mary Teresa and it was like a hand reaching out just as I was going under for good. I had begun to have contempt for myself. I mean for the wrong reasons. She is still the only safe harbor for me."

"Lydia, where were you when you left the car at the garage?"

"Didn't Sister Mary Teresa tell you?"

"No."

"I guess I'm not surprised."

"Will you tell me?"

"I talked with someone who persuaded me to come back here. You wouldn't know him."

"Your lawyer, Bill Dunning?"

"No! No. He doesn't want to know where I am."

"I'm glad you're concerned about him."

"But he would have to turn me in if I went to him. He would be in professional trouble if he didn't."

There seemed no comparable professional trouble Kim could appeal to in the case of Emtee Dempsey. The old nun had stuck her own neck out and was going to have to pay the price of her hubris. That could not be blamed on Lydia. Emtee Dempsey could never be persuaded to do anything she thought was the wrong thing.

They were interrupted by the appearance of a triumphant Emtee Dempsey in the doorway. The old nun inhaled deeply before speaking.

"Mr. Fenwick has made a statement to the police, Lydia."

"What did he say?"

"The point, my dear, is that he has put it on the public record that you were with him when that unfortunate woman was drowned. I think you need fear no further persecution on that score."

Emtee Dempsey fairly glowed as she said this.

"It was Mr. Fenwick who persuaded you to return here?" Kim asked.

"Yes," Lydia said, distractedly, her attention still on the old nun. "What exactly did he say?"

"That you and he were talking together for more than an hour. Remembering old times."

Lydia looked away. "I've become good at that."

An hour and a half later, Bill Dunning, Mr. Rush, Kim, Joyce, and Lydia sat in the living room listening to Sister Mary Teresa explain matters to Richard Moriarity, who had been summoned by Kim with the promise that he would find Lydia Hopkins at the house on Walton Street.

"How long have you been here?" Richard demanded of Lydia.

Emtee Dempsey said smoothly, "She came directly here from her conversation with Mr. Fenwick. He wisely recommended she come to me. As you know, Richard, we corresponded while Lydia was being held in prison."

"Where were you before talking with Fenwick?"

"She was out of the state," Emtee Dempsey answered.

"Where, Indiana?"

"Richard, why don't we keep to the essentials? A warrant was unwisely issued for Lydia's arrest in the matter of the drowning of Dolores Merrill. Mr. Fenwick's statement has revealed that for the nonsense it is. We have gathered here to get that warrant rescinded."

"It is still in force, Sister, and I am officially and formally arresting Lydia Hopkins. I cannot presume on the judgment of a court. Sure, it looks as if Fenwick's statement helps her in the Merrill case. But what about the other murders?"

What Adam Fenwick said, in its entirety, Kim had to piece together from what Richard said then, what Katherine said when she came calling later, and from the TV news. The last, of course, impressed its images on her mind.

Fenwick was a lanky, suntanned man with a white mustache separated in the center as if to match the slight separation between his front teeth.

"Maybe this is suppression of evidence, I don't know. Maybe I should get a lawyer before I say all this, but I am sick and tired of sitting by and seeing a lovely lady persecuted the way Lydia Hopkins has been. So if I'm running a risk, so be it. At my age, what can they do to me?"

Sitting next to Kim, Emtee Dempsey harrumphed. For such a suntanned, obviously healthy man to lay claim to the prerogatives of age seemed an abuse to the old nun, though the truth was Fenwick was not three years younger than she. The verdant fairways and make-believe problems of golf had given him a long life, one in which few psychic demands had been made on him, to say nothing of physical exertion. Not that Emtee Dempsey objected to grown men, and women, earning a living by playing the games of children.

"Most of what people do is little more than a game. Take insurance. . . ." And she was off, likening life insurance to Lotto, with Lotto not only a better bargain but less solemn in its claims on players.

Fenwick's account was of course punctuated and interrupted by the allegedly probing questions of a television reporter whose grasp of the facts concerning the murders of Lydia's husband and daughter was not firm. The emphasis of the interview was on recent events when the important part of what the old pro had to say bore on the past.

The great revelation was that Fenwick had recently come upon Lydia's missing golf clubs, which apparently had been in the pro shop when her husband and daughter were slain and had languished there for years until they had been sent along with other items in the shop to Fenwick. Everyone remembered how annoyed the police were to find Lydia's locker all but empty when they searched it.

"It didn't dawn on anyone then that the clubs might be in the shop. Don't ask me why. It didn't enter my mind. A couple months ago, Byron, my successor . . ." Fenwick's voice trailed away and his face hardened. Retirement was hard but he seemed to have doubts about Byron's ability to succeed him. Bobby Byron had finally insisted that Fenwick remove everything from the pro shop and delivered it all to the Fenwick garage. "That's where I found her clubs. In my garage."

"I see," the interviewer said, not seeing at all what a set of golf clubs had to do with anything.

"Well, yesterday I told Lydia about those clubs and we agreed they proved she hadn't gotten rid of them the way the prosecutor suggested in the trial."

And the fact that Lydia was with Fenwick when Dolores Merrill was killed provided a needed alibi.

The conference in the house on Walton Street ended in a compromise. Bill Dunning and Richard called Monday, the prosecutor, and set up a meeting for later that afternoon. Lydia Hopkins would be there, Monday insisted on that; he had been the target of incessant flak from Carrillo about Lydia's whereabouts and, he said, he wanted photographers present to prove he had located her before lifting the warrant. Emtee Dempsey did not like such catering to the male ego, but Raymond insisted, and in the event Kim was to accompany Lydia.

"I do not want one of my postulants going about unattended," Emtee Dempsey said primly. As if by unspoken agreement, they all observed half a minute's silence after that remark. Lydia Hopkins stared across the room at her protectress with wide, unbelieving eyes. Well might she wonder how she had gained such a champion, Kim thought.

The scene in Monday's office was what has come to be described as a media event. From the moment they entered, Kim had the sense that whatever was said or done was being said or done for the record rather than anything else. With newspaper photographers jostling with television newscam operators, Raymond Monday, bathed in artificial light, addressed the greedy lenses before him.

"The people of this city have been led to believe that my office is unable to act on an arrest warrant because the police cannot locate the principals. It is in large part to stifle such nonsense that I have called you here to announce that the warrant for the arrest of Lydia Hopkins as a suspect in the murder of Dolores Merrill has been revoked. This woman is, of course, Lydia Hopkins."

Those cameras that had not already been concentrating on Lydia now swung to her. Lydia seemed to shrink in her chair before this concentrated attention and it was at this moment, when all eyes were on her, that Monday made his extraordinary statement. The reaction was delayed, but then the very walls of the room seemed to converge on Raymond Monday. For a moment his expression indicated he thought he had spoiled his dramatic opportunity, but now he had a second chance and he fixed a steely gaze on the television lenses.

"In the light of evidence recently obtained by my office, I have drawn up a new indictment against Lydia Hopkins, a charge of first-degree murder committed against Jeffrey Hopkins and Laura Hopkins."

In the ensuing pandemonium, Lydia Hopkins might have been the calmest person in the room as Kim struggled to keep close to her. She crouched beside the chair and Lydia's hand swiftly enclosed hers. At that moment in the courthouse, in Monday's office, Kim was vividly aware of the powerful governmental machinery that would be set in motion in order to put Lydia back in prison. Meanwhile, reporters were shouting questions, demanding to know what the new evidence was.

Monday was obviously torn between refusing to say and using this chance to restore his tattered public image. He did not hesitate long.

"Evidence that should have been found and used at the time of the original trial has been discovered by my office and, with it, I have no doubt I will obtain a conviction that will not be overturned."

"Is that a crack at Carrillo?"

"Call it an expression of pride in the current conduct of this office."

"What is the evidence?"

Monday made them beg; the question became an almost chant, but finally he lifted his hand.

"Her golf clubs," he said. "Lydia Hopkins's golf clubs."

At these words, Lydia squeezed Kim's hand painfully. She shut her eyes, pressed her lips tightly together, and began to nod her head. Then she let go of Kim's hand and got slowly to her feet. Her manner silenced the room, and everyone, including a suddenly apprehensive Monday, looked at her.

"I would like to say something."

Bill Dunning, shaking his head, shouted, "Lydia, no! I don't want—"

Her right hand made a lazy movement of dismissal and Dunning was elbowed back by an enormous photographer.

"I shall plead guilty to the indictment," Lydia said.

A groan went up from Dunning.

"I shall plead guilty for two reason. First, because I am. Second, to avoid having to go through another trial. I am ready to go back to prison."

Kim decided later that she would never again be critical of the confusing accounts of eyewitnesses. She had often been praised by Emtee Dempsey for the thoroughness of the reports she brought back to Walton Street and she had taken pride in the fact that this was true. But she had never before felt so much part of what she tried to describe as on that occasion in Raymond Monday's office when Lydia Hopkins told the world that she had killed her husband and daughter.

Another thing she decided was that her opinion of the working press had been irreparably damaged on that occasion. She had seen the tenacity and viciousness with which reporters sometimes pursue politicians, but politicians have freely chosen to expose themselves to such indignity. Lydia was like a cornered animal and the press a wolf pack that has caught the scent of blood. Kim could give no coherent account of how Lydia had been safely removed from the room. It was almost possible to be grateful that she was in a cell now and out of reach of those ravenous reporters. But Lydia had managed to say one last thing to Kim before she was taken from the room.

"I'm sorry, Kim. Tell Sister Mary Teresa that."

That message was the worst with which Kim had ever returned to Walton Street. She could not honestly say that she was surprised at this final admission of guilt on Lydia's part. It was the only thing consistent with what she herself had learned about Lydia and her marriage during these past few days. The difficulty lay in the further significance of the message.

It meant that Sister Mary Teresa had been thoroughly mistaken about Lydia Hopkins.

It meant that Sister Mary Teresa now ran the risk of public ridicule. She had promised to prove innocent a woman who had now publicly confessed her guilt.

For the first time, Sister Mary Teresa was manifestly wrong, and there were altogether too many people who were not likely to let her forget it.

Beginning with Kim's brother, Richard Moriarity.

Who could blame him? How many times had he been forced to eat his words and acknowledge that he had been wrong because of Sister Mary Teresa? He would need heroic virtue to pass up this longed-for opportunity to give the old nun a taste of her own medicine.

It was Kim's reluctance to face Sister Mary Teresa with this turn of events that made her detour past Katherine's apartment. Katherine listened, a thumb and index finger tugging down the corners of her generous mouth. She stared out the window to where Lake Michigan and the heavens met in a blurred unity at the horizon.

"I suppose it had to happen sometime. But do you know, Sister Kimberly, I honestly believed it never would. What a run that woman has had!"

"I don't think I can face her alone."

"No, I couldn't ask you to do that. After all, I've known her far longer than you have. But before we go, let's get all the factual matters clarified."

So Kim had a dry run of making her report to Emtee Dempsey, telling Katherine of the scene in Monday's office. The veteran reporter did not object to Kim's description of the antics of the press when Monday sprang his surprise.

"Golf clubs. Dear God, Fenwick thought he was helping her when he produced that bag of clubs. What evidence did they provide?"

Monday had not said.

"Surely he was asked?"

Kim found that she could not answer yes or no to that,
but Katherine stopped her apologies.

"Given the chaos you so vividly describe, I'm surprised
you can remember anything that was said." She reached
for her phone. "Let me see what I can find out."

What Katherine found out was that Lydia's sand
wedge was found to have both blood and hair that
matched those of her husband and daughter. The long-
sought bludgeoning weapon had been found in Lydia's
golf bag, which had been languishing in Fenwick's garage
all this time. Despite the lapse of time, there was no doubt
of the match between the stains on the forged steel club
head and the other evidence that was still in the possession
of the police.

Katherine intervened with that factual data when Kim had
brought her account to the point of Monday's announcement of the new indictment and the new evidence. They
were in the study and the old nun was sitting forward ea-
gerly, her elbows on her desk, her hands pressing into her
cheeks as she followed with rapt attention what Kim had
said and what Katherine was now saying. The blue eyes
behind the oval rimless glasses were bright with excitement
and she seemed to be breathing more rapidly than normal
through her half-opened mouth. As Katherine explained
about the golf club, Emtee Dempsey's hands left her
cheeks. She brought them together, then pressed her fingertips against her now-closed lips. In other circumstances, Kim would have thought the old nun was
suppressing a smile.

Katherine said, "You may remember that those missing golf clubs were made much of in the first trial."

"On the supposition that a golf club could have been the instrument the killer used."

"That's right."

"And they think that proves Lydia guilty!"

Katherine looked at Kim. There was no point in postponing it any further.

"Sister, there is more. After the prosecutor made his remarks, Lydia spoke."

"I'm not surprised."

"Sister, please. Lydia admitted her guilt. She admitted killing her husband and daughter."

The old nun's face now had no more expression than a peach, but her eyes darted brightly from Kim to Katherine and back. Then she slammed her hands down on the desk.

"Good!" she cried. She nodded vigorously and then let out an enormous sigh. "Thank God. I had hoped it could be done more easily, but this will more than do."

"Do what, Sister?" Katherine's voice was soothing but unsteady, as if she were addressing a child.

"Why, vindicate my faith in Lydia, of course. Dear friends, we have succeeded."

"Succeeded!" Kim cried.

Emtee Dempsey sat back and looked patiently at Kim. "Sister, what has been the point of our efforts?"

"To prove Lydia innocent. Everything I brought back to you undermined that assumption. Lydia's behavior undermined the assumption. And now she has announced to the world that she is guilty."

Sister Mary Teresa waved her hand and Kim realized this was the gesture Lydia had mimicked in silencing her lawyer, William Dunning. "Our aim, Sister Kimberly, was to force the prosecutor to leave Lydia alone by providing him with the real murderer."

114

"Sister—"

"And we are now about to do that."

"Lydia has confessed, Sister. She has admitted she did those things."

"Of course, she did. And that means only one thing. We have the means to identify the murderer. That is why Lydia made her absurd confession. The question now is, Who is she protecting?"

"Protecting." Katherine shook her head but her face was a mixture of pity and admiration for Emtee Dempsey's reluctance to go down without a struggle.

"What other explanation can there be for an innocent person saying that she committed two brutal murders? Lydia hitherto has always, in public and in private, maintained her innocence."

"So she confessed in order to spare the real murderer?"

Emtee Dempsey nodded in a preoccupied way.

"Then she must know who the real murderer is. Did she tell you that, perhaps?"

The old nun looked quickly at Katherine. "I know you never shared my belief that Lydia is innocent. And it was only a belief, I assure you. No, she did not tell me who killed her husband and daughter because she did not know. She was reluctant to suggest possibilities even when she agreed that the only way the matter was likely to be put behind her once and for all was to have the murderer apprehended." She turned to Kim. "What was said in Mr. Monday's office thus becomes of supreme importance. You heard everything that Lydia heard and what she heard both told her who the murderer was and prompted her to confess in order to protect that person. Sister Kimberly, I want you to turn your considerable powers of recall on what went on in that office this afternoon. Everything and anything you can remember I must know."

Kim thought that it would have been easier if Sister

Mary Teresa had been crushed by this turn of events, certainly easier for her. But to have to continue this conversation with a suddenly rejuvenated Emtee Dempsey acting for all the world as if she had been given good news rather than bad required of Kim something she had never before needed in dealing with the old nun—the suppression of pity. The mighty had fallen and would not admit it, and that meant the old nun had deteriorated far more than a mere misuse of her mind entailed. It was her mind itself that revealed its weakness. Against all the evidence, against Lydia's public confession, Emtee Dempsey not only retained her belief in Lydia's innocence, her confidence seemed to have increased.

And Katherine was no help. After Kim had delivered what should have been the coup de grace, only to have Emtee Dempsey incredibly conclude that now her belief in Lydia's innocence was all but proven, Katherine fell into league with her old friend, exploring the new avenues allegedly opened up, as if she sincerely believed there was some basis for Sister Mary Teresa's all-but-maniacal glee.

"You will remember, Katherine, whom William Dunning offered as a prime suspect in the murders of Jeffrey and Laura Hopkins. Adam Fenwick."

That was true.

"And it was Fenwick Lydia went to see the day she pretended I had telephoned her at the lake."

"How could he have known where she was?"

"He didn't. Sister Kimberly was right. The call itself was fabricated, not simply that I had called. She feigned a call in order to have an excuse to come back to town and talk with Fenwick."

"Who advised her to return here?" Kim said, hating herself. There was something immoral about encouraging

Emtee Dempsey to believe that there was something still to be discovered.

"Precisely."

"Are you suggesting that Fenwick murdered Jeffrey and Laura Hopkins?" Katherine asked.

"You're right, of course. That does suggest itself."

"Dolores Merrill was a neighbor of Fenwick's."

Kim could not take any more. She left the study and went into the kitchen, where she heard the murmur of the television in the basement apartment. She continued down to where Joyce was hunched before the set watching the "Thursday Night Fights" on ESPN. There was a bowl of popcorn on the floor between her shoes and a crushed diet Pepsi can in her hand. On the screen two bleeding boxers pummeled each other mercilessly. Joyce glanced at Kim, and lifted her hand.

"Final minute of the final round."

Kim waited, keeping her eyes off the set. She found it hard to imagine how a civilized country could permit such a sport. Joyce argued that it was a sign of civilization and cheered the resurgence of boxing on television. The round ended and Joyce turned down the sound.

"They have to call it a draw," she said.

"Joyce, Lydia admitted killing her husband and child."

"I know. It was on. Do you think she did?"

"Joyce, I was there."

"I mean, did the murders."

"You're as bad as Emtee Dempsey! She thinks Lydia's confession proves she didn't do it."

"She's protecting someone?"

"Have you and Sister talked about this?"

"I know how her mind works. It makes sense. But what made her say that now?"

Kim gave up. She wanted to explain to Joyce what

this defeat would mean for Emtee Dempsey. There was no way it could be kept secret that the old nun had vowed to prove Lydia innocent. Not even Lydia pretended that anymore. Indeed, Lydia least of all. Kim went back upstairs to the study as if she were Alice returning to Wonderland.

Seven

❖

T he pool between Adam Fenwick's house and the sixteenth fairway seemed to be filled with a combination of lemon and lime Jell-O that had not set. From where Kim sat, she could look up the curve of the fairway and see a series of such pools, among them that in which Dolores Merrill had died. With the nail of the little finger of his right hand Fenwick traced the line of his white mustache.

"My great fear is that some child will wander in here, fall in the pool, and drown. The insurance company calls it an attractive hazard. As opposed to that bunker, I suppose." He pointed toward the fairway. "That's the reason for this fence, by the way."

There was a steel cyclone fence, blue in color, surrounding the pool. Looking through it gave the world a rhomboid aspect.

"Do you still golf?" Kim asked.

The fingernail sought refuge in his lower teeth as he

dipped his head to look at her over his glasses. "Young lady, golf is a game you can play until the day you die. My father did. He had a massive heart attack after hitting a perfect approach shot to the eighth green on a course near Sarasota. That's the way I hope to go. Preferably after I putt out, however." He smiled. "Do you golf?"

"I haven't for years."

"Go back to it."

Kim sipped the soft drink he had insisted she have. It was the day after Lydia had confessed to the murders of her husband and child. It was two days since the drowning of Dolores Merrill. It should have been easier than it was proving to be to get Fenwick onto one or other of those topics. The allusion to Dolores had not worked. Maybe being subtle was not the way.

"Were you shocked by Lydia's confession?"

"I don't believe it for a moment."

"Oh, she said it. I was there."

"I mean I don't believe it's true. She could never have done such a thing."

"You're very loyal."

He finally lighted the cigarette he had been holding un-lit since they sat down beside his pool. Had he wanted that cloud of smoke through which to scrutinize her?

"I'm told you spent time talking with personnel at the clubhouse."

"I was looking for leads to prove Lydia's innocence."

"Why should that concern you?"

He really seemed interested when she told him about Sister Mary Teresa and their community on Walton Street. The fact that the old nun had corresponded with Lydia while she was in prison impressed him.

"I never visited her there. She didn't want to see people, I guess. I know I could not have borne it."

"Did you write to her?"

120

He removed ashes from the end of his cigarette with the same fingernail he had used to groom his mustache. "What did they tell you at the club?"

"Oh, all kinds of things."

"I meant about me and Lydia."

"I'd be interested in your account, if you care to give it to me. Give it to Sister Mary Teresa, that is. All these inquiries are made for her."

"I've never confessed to a nun before."

"Are you a Catholic?"

A rueful little laugh escaped him and he looked out over the golf course. "I was raised one. Am I one now? I don't see how I can say yes. Do you know what separated me from the church?"

"What?"

"Golf. Golfing on Sundays. I got out of the habit of going to Mass. There was no dramatic rejection. It was not even like falling out of love. It was more like gradually forgetting someone you no longer see." He sighed. Was he thinking of not having visited Lydia while she was in prison? "At my age there are so many people I will never see again."

"Do you still golf on Sundays?"

"Are you trying to convert me?"

"There are Saturday-night Masses now."

"The best of both worlds?"

On another occasion, she would have pursued that topic for its own sake. But the state of Fenwick's soul was not the reason for her visit.

"You were going to tell me about you and Lydia."

"I loved her."

"I see."

"It was completely innocent, I assure you. She was ages younger than I. She reminded me of a girl I have always

121

thought I should have married and didn't. I lost her the way I lost religion. She didn't golf."

"Did Lydia golf?"

"If she had she wouldn't have reminded me of Sarah. But then she took it up. As, she assured me, Sarah would have."

"Did you ever marry?"

"Twice. I buried them both. Sister Mary Teresa could tell you the actuarial unlikelihood of that. They both golfed too, wisely but not well."

"But Sarah didn't."

"No. After the Hopkinses joined the club and Lydia reminded me so forcefully of her, I made an effort to discover if Sarah was still alive. It is not easy to trace a woman after a lapse of years. First, you must learn the name of the man she married, not as easy as you might think. A second marriage makes her even harder to discover."

"Did you find her?"

"No. So I transferred to Lydia all my romantic longing for the girl who got away."

"Did she know that?"

"She thought it was my pitch, my line, but it intrigued her nonetheless. We spent happy hours together, at the club, always public, always innocent. Just outside the pro shop, there is a little terrace, a few tables. We would sit there, have a drink, talk. I loved her. As a daughter, perhaps, as a sort of imaginary character. Do you know Henry James?"

"The novelist?"

"His novel *The Awkward Age* reminded me of Lydia and myself."

"I never imagined Henry James would be read by a golf pro."

"How many golf pros have you known?"

"None." She laughed. She could easily imagine Lydia sitting with this man, having a drink, just talking. After a few minutes, Kim had forgotten how handsome Fenwick was and become fascinated by his manner. Of course, his statement that he had been brought up a Catholic created an affinity of sorts. But there was an easy charm about him she succumbed to easily. Kim decided Sister Mary Teresa would have to meet Fenwick. The thought brought her back to her purpose in being here.

"Why would Lydia say she had killed her husband and daughter if she didn't?"

His glasses lifted when he wrinkled his nose. "That's a question I'd like to ask her."

"Why don't you?"

He put his cigarette out carefully, then pitched it over the fence onto the lawn.

"She came to see me the other day, you know."

"I know."

"Once before she came to me and shortly after was arrested. I told her I'm not good luck for her. She said she didn't believe in luck. Maybe she does now."

"Why did she come see you the other day?"

He smiled sadly. "To tell me that she wanted to stay with you on Walton Street. She wanted my blessing." He said it with wonderment. "We always got along very well. We could talk for hours. Benny, the boy in the pro shop, once said Lydia and I talked even when neither of us said anything. I didn't realize how much I had missed her until I saw her again."

"Have you been in touch with her since she was arrested?"

"Is Bill Dunning still her lawyer?"

"Yes."

"I don't think he would let me near her."

"Why not?"

"He might give you a dozen reasons, but not the true one. He is half in love with Lydia himself and cannot admit it. Imagine losing the case when he felt that way about her."

Was he suggesting a broken man, haunted by failure? That was not the William Dunning Kim had met. She told Fenwick this.

"You should have seen him just after the trial. He was in a state of shock for months. Two weeks after the sentencing, he made a hole in one on number seven and just walked off the course. It didn't mean a damned thing to him. A hole in one!"

Kim supposed golf could provide a measure of mental unease.

"Besides, if I had kept my mouth shut, Lydia would not be in trouble again. I thought producing those clubs would help her!" He shook his head and studied the smoldering tip of his cigarette, tobacco and paper transforming themselves into ash and smoke. Adam Fenwick seemed to taste more ashes than smoke.

"Sister Mary Teresa wanted me to ask about the transfer of Lydia's golf clubs to your garage. Where is your garage, by the way?"

"In that low building across the road. All the units have garages over there."

"Someone brought the clubs here?"

"That's right. Benny. He still works in the pro shop. You wouldn't have talked with him."

"Why?"

Fenwick touched his head. "He worked for me, Byron kept him on, thank God. I don't know what else he could do."

"When did you retire?"

"It's almost five years." He said it as if he expected her to contest it.

124

"When exactly were the clubs brought to you?"

"It wasn't just clubs, although there were five bags of them. Other stuff too, plaques, lesser trophies and mementos, my personal records of tournaments, that kind of thing, office stuff."

"Are the other things he brought still in your garage?"

He looked at his watch. "Maybe. But not for long. I donated it to a yard sale."

"Whose?"

"At Jane Flannery's parish. It was when I was looking over what I might have for her that I found Lydia's clubs." He shook his head. He was caressing another unlighted cigarette. "My only thought was that those clubs would clear up one of the points Carrillo kept making in the trial. Why did she clean out her locker? Where were her golf clubs?"

"And at the time of the trial they were in your garage?"

He nodded. "Isn't that a kick? And then I turn them over with a big splash and look what happens. I wish now I had thrown them away. Or just let Jane have them. But I thought I would ride to the defense of Lydia. I might very well have put her back in prison for good."

"Why exactly did Lydia come to see you the day Dolores Merrill drowned?"

"You sound as if you're connecting Lydia's being here with Dolores's drowning. Poor Dolores."

"Who do you suppose was responsible for her death?"

"God only knows." He pointed beyond the fence in the direction of the golf course. "The club is private but it's an easy thing to get onto the course. I don't mean to golf. That is monitored pretty closely by rangers. If they don't recognize someone, they always stop and inquire. What I mean is that these condominiums are very vulnerable to prowlers coming in off the golf course. When these places were planned I think we all thought that those who lived here would be surrounded by the otherworldly peace of the golf course. The real world ceases to exist as soon as you tee up your ball, you know. Golf can be a necessity of life for some. In any case, I suppose some maniac came into Dolores's yard off the fairway."

"A member?"

"Good God, no. A vagrant, a trespasser, some pervert. Not that Dolores was sexually assaulted."

Not a line Kim cared to pursue. She looked at the fairway, the trees lining it, the golden sandtraps randomly set throughout the green expanse. A large tractor mower moved majestically down the fairway spinning blades of grass into the shimmering air. The smell of freshly cut grass was fragrant in their nostrils.

"You must come visit us on Walton Street."

He smiled noncommittally. "Will you be seeing Lydia?"

"I think so."

"Tell her I am thinking of her."

"Did she come here to tell you she wanted to become one of us? Sister Mary Teresa took it quite seriously."

"Don't you?"

"It's not an easy thing to be a nun."

"You carry it off rather well."

"But I have a vocation."

"And Lydia does not?"

"That's not for me to say."

He looked at her in silence. "Maybe that is another reason I stopped being a Catholic. I don't think women should withdraw behind a veil of ignorance. I think women ought to marry."

Kim overcame the impulse to answer that. Let Sister Mary Teresa explain it to him if he ever came to Walton Street.

*   *   *

William Dunning was reluctant to see her in the first
place, but when she mentioned Adam Fenwick he grew
visibly impatient.

"Why couldn't he have kept his nose out of this?"

"He thought he was helping."

"Helping!" A furrow formed between his brows.

"He told me you once made a hole in one."

This caught Dunning off guard. He didn't know how to
react for a moment, but then he said, musingly, "Imagine
remembering something like that. But I suppose that's
what golf pros do remember. He would know all our
handicaps too."

"Handicaps?"

He laughed. "A technical term. The average number of
strokes over par, divided by— It's very complicated, I'm
not sure I understand it myself. Yes, I once made a hole in
one on number seven."

"And then just walked off the course?"

"Yes." The furrow returned. "It wasn't long after the
trial. I felt guilty playing a game while my client was in
prison. And then to make a hole in one!"

"Fenwick still thinks Lydia is innocent."

"Hasn't he heard what she blurted out in Monday's office?"

"Sister Mary Teresa doesn't believe she did it either."

"It would be nice if we could prove that."

"She intends to. She holds that the reason Lydia confessed is to protect someone else."

"Who?"

"Sister is not yet ready to say."

His mouth opened slightly during this exchange, as if he
were trying to discern whether Kim was serious. He was
silent for a moment, then got up from behind his desk and

walked to a window. He was a silhouette when he turned to her.

"I'm trying to think of a way to put this delicately. I have a great deal of respect for Sister Mary Teresa. I understand she is a first-rate historian. She is a pleasant conversationalist. She has been very decent to Lydia Hopkins. I appreciate that as Lydia's lawyer. I appreciate that as Lydia's friend. But this is not a game played in a convent parlor. It is a serious matter, a matter of life or death, and it will be decided in a courtroom according to very formal procedures. The way things look now, I have almost no chance of winning an acquittal for Lydia. I will not permit her to plead guilty. I frankly don't know how I can prevent a verdict of guilty. Quite apart from her statement in public that she is guilty, there are those goddamn golf clubs." He brought his hand down in what had to be a painful way on the windowsill.

He came back to his desk and sat. "And old Adam Fenwick sits out there by his pool remembering holes in one."

"You once suggested to Sister Mary Teresa that Fenwick might have committed those murders."

"Did I say that? I hope she didn't take me seriously."

"Why did you say it at all?"

"He was nuts about her. The way old men sometimes are about young women. They used to spend hours together at the club. Talking. That's probably what they were doing the other day when she visited him. Any grievances she had with Jeff he would be sure to share. If she had motive, so did he, by derivation. But let me make clear now what I should have made clear when I spoke to Sister Mary Teresa. That is the airiest of speculation. It has not a grain of support in anything like evidence. It's a guess."

"A hunch?"

He gave it some thought. "Not even quite that."

128

"Would she do this to protect him?"

"From what? Do you know how old he is?"

"No."

"He is seventy-nine years old."

"That's hard to believe. Didn't he retire just five years ago?"

"At the age of seventy-five. And he can still golf at his age. He will be eighty shortly. Why would Lydia, with her whole life ahead of her, sacrifice herself for a man with one foot in the grave?" He looked at her closely. "Is that Sister Mary Teresa's theory?"

"No."

"Did she want you to ask me that?"

"The thought occurred to me just now. I had no idea he was so old. I came to ask you something quite specific."

"Go ahead."

"You said once that Jeffrey Hopkins had hired a detective to follow Lydia."

"He did."

"How can I contact that detective?"

"Why would you want to do that?"

"Because Sister Mary Teresa asked me to."

"All right. Why would *she* want to do that?"

"You must ask her. What is the detective's name?"

"Looking him up only makes sense if you are gathering evidence *against* Lydia."

"You know better than that. Sister Mary Teresa has never wavered in her conviction that Lydia is innocent. She is more than ever convinced of it now. She wants to identify the one Lydia is protecting. It's the only defense left."

"The one she is protecting being the murderer?"

"Yes."

"Did you explain all that to Fenwick?"

"Why do you ask?"

"I just wonder how gallant he is. If you put an idea like that in his head, he's liable to telephone the police again."

"We didn't talk about it in any detail."

"Too bad." The furrow in his forehead was symmetrical with the dimple in his chin.

"Are you serious?"

"Sister, right now just about anything that would muddy the waters would be welcome to me. I have half a mind to put the idea into Fenwick's head myself."

"I don't think you would."

"I said half a mind."

"Who was the detective?"

"I'd hoped you'd forgotten about her."

"Her!"

"Beverly John. I've got her address here somewhere. I think she's in Oak Park."

He could not find it in the book he took from his desk drawer, but his secretary, a bony woman in a tailored suit who seemed to walk in clouds of perfume, brought in a card she had removed from her Rolodex.

"Let Sister jot that down."

Kim had not identified herself as a nun when she came to the office and, as she noted down the address and phone number of Beverly John, she was aware in peripheral vision of the secretary's startled gaze on her.

GEM Services was located across from the Brick Yard Mall in one of those spin-off mini-malls that gather like cowbirds around the grosser beast. The simile was stated by the small-boned, gray-haired woman with oversize glasses on the other side of the desk. Beverly John.

"What's a cowbird?"

"You're a city girl."

"If that's the test."

"Just what are you?" Her head tipped to one side as if to get a better view. "I can't place you."

"I'm a nun."

Her mouth popped open but there was a delay before a dry laugh emerged. "Honest?"

Kim had to check herself or she would have answered, "Honest Injun." Beverly John would never see sixty again, her office was as nondescript as herself, but there was an undeniable air of make-believe. Kim had already established that GEM Services kept an eye on people their clients wanted an eye kept on. In short, they followed them around. It was the essence of a childish game, the unobserved observer, the child behind the drape or under the bed or hidden among the coats in a closet. With some reluctance, Kim explained to Beverly John about the Order of Martha and Mary, the house on Walton Street, Emtee Dempsey, Lydia Hopkins.

"Aha! Lydia Hopkins. I once . . . ." She stopped. "But of course that's why you're here."

"Jeffrey Hopkins once hired you to follow his wife."

A nod of the gray head.

"What was his reason?"

"Do you know what GEM stands for? It's an acronym."

"What?"

"Green-eyed monster. That's the reason, nine out of ten times. People think private detectives are hired to gather evidence for a divorce. Apart from the fact that that is no longer necessary, it misses the whole point of an operation like this one. Only people in love hire me, jealous people."

"And Jeffrey Hopkins was in love with his wife?"

"Is the Pope Polish? Sorry."

Kim nodded, not knowing what else to do. "I suppose everything you find is confidential."

"Why don't you ask me if I know anything about Lydia Hopkins that would help her at the present time?"

"All right."

"Ask me. For the record."

"Are you recording this?"

"Only here." She put a finger to her temple as if she were going to shoot herself.

"Do you know anything about Lydia Hopkins that would help her now?"

"Let's have a cup of coffee."

It was already made, thick as molasses in a pot that must have been brewing darkly since the crack of dawn. The coffee formed beads on Kim's tongue. Beverly John made smacking sounds involving the roof of her mouth, an approving verdict.

"I like strong coffee. Now, about Jeffrey Hopkins and his wife."

Kim had the odd sense that she was Emtee Dempsey and Beverly John was herself, reporting on an errand of inquiry. The picture of a hesitant, embarrassed Jeffrey Hopkins on his first visit, the circumlocutions he used to say he wanted his wife followed to see if she were seeing another man—all that was deftly and vividly portrayed by Beverly John.

"He had no one specific in mind, he said, but that is a common, and annoying, claim. And, as it usually does, it caused us to waste time. For example, when our first report went into detail on the amount of time Mrs. Hopkins spent with the golf pro at the country club, Mr. Hopkins dismissed it as unimportant. He was certain there was someone, months after it seemed clear to me there was not."

"No one?"

"Nothing untoward at all."

"I was told at the country club that she would often, almost daily, drop her daughter off there and disappear."

"She didn't disappear from us. Two days a week she worked as a volunteer with cancer patients at Our Lady Hospital. Under her maiden name. One day a week, she prayed."

"Prayed?"

"She sat and knelt, alternately, for an hour and a half in Saint John of God parish before a statue of the Virgin Mary that was reported to be crying."

Kim sat back as if she had been pushed. "What did her husband say when you told him that?"

"He would hardly listen to anything that showed her innocent. What he wanted was proof she was guilty. Why did he need to punish himself? I see that a lot. The human heart is a mechanism with a lot of crossed wires."

"A volunteer worker? A woman who engaged in prolonged prayer? None of that matches what I've heard about her."

"And what have you heard? Other than the famous ashtray incident, that is."

"Don't you think it happened?"

"He threw a tantrum in the dining room, accusing her of all kinds of things, and he was smoking. His cigarette had burned down. She tossed him an ashtray. Underarm. That's all that happened."

"And once she banged her car repeatedly into his, in their driveway. The neighbors—"

"Look, he was constantly confronting her with his baseless accusations. If not in public, then at home. Wouldn't she want to escape that? Wouldn't she be in an emotional state when she left? Did you ever want to bang a car that pinned you into a parking place? That episode, whatever

133

really happened, doesn't tell you much about Lydia Hopkins."

"Why wasn't all this brought out at the trial?"

Beverly John shrugged. "I called her lawyer. I left messages. I wrote him a letter I could show you, indicating the kind of character-witness stuff I had. The response was a chilly one, the idea being that testimony from a private detective would only worsen matters."

"But the hospital! He could have looked into that himself."

"Well, not quite. I wasn't that open-handed. I didn't give him all the details. You see, I hadn't been paid yet."

"You weren't paid?"

"I was owed money. I was still on the case."

The significance of that remark did not come immediately, but Beverly John waited until it did.

"Are you saying you were still following Lydia at the time of the murders?"

The gray head nodded once and then she brought her mug to her mouth and kept her eyes on Kim as she sipped coffee.

"Was she being watched when she came out of the house and drove away on the afternoon her husband and child were killed?"

"Yes."

"You mean, you actually followed her from the house?"

"GEM Services did. I didn't handle the Hopkins account personally."

"Who did?"

"Mildred Pilsudski."

"Is she still with you?"

Beverly John's expression altered slightly and she shook her head. "Mildred passed away just yesterday. It was in the papers. The coroner's verdict was suicide. In her garage, the motor running. My gas." She shook her head again.

"Were you ever paid for your investigation?"

"Eventually Mr. Dunning acknowledged the debt and paid. That is when I sent him all the reports."

"He has your reports?"

"He paid for them, he gets them. Acting for the heir of my client, that is. Which he was."

"You've been very helpful."

"And confusing?"

"That, too."

"I would like to meet Sister Mary Teresa sometime."

"I think she is going to want to meet you."

"Is that all you want to ask me about?"

"You've been very helpful."

"It's not altogether unpleasant to speak to someone whose motive is not jealousy."

It seemed ironic that she was getting this different and more congenial picture of Lydia only after Lydia had confessed to those awful murders. Emtee Dempsey's theory now looked like a good deal more than wishful thinking. The trouble lay in proving it. There were two requirements of the theory. Someone with motive and opportunity to kill Jeffrey and Laura Hopkins. And someone Lydia would want to shield from the consequences of murdering her husband and child. Did anyone fulfill one of those requirements, let alone both?

"There is a third requirement," Emtee Dempsey said blandly, when Kim made her observation. "The same person must be responsible for the death of Dolores Merrill."

"Good Lord." Katherine held her martini almost at arm's length, having considerably lowered its level with her first taste.

"Indeed," Emtee Dempsey said. "The first step is of course routine. Excluding people."

"You make it sound as if you have a lineup of possibilities," Kim said.

"We must know the whereabouts of William Dunning, Mr. Fenwick, the personnel at the club who misled us so about her character. . . . Which reminds me, I want to talk with Jane Flannery."

"It sounds as if you would be better advised to talk to Beverly John."

"A splendid idea, Katherine."

"She charges for her services."

"Oh, I'm sure that any expenses that are incurred extricating Lydia from this mess will be happily taken care of."

"I would very much like to talk to Lydia now," Kim said.

"Sister Kimberly, you are reading my mind. Do you think you could get in to see her today?"

It was going on nine in the evening. Katherine made a call that established the impossibility of seeing Lydia until the following day. But a time for Kim's visit was set: 10:00 A.M. the next day.

"Another favor, Katherine," Emtee Dempsey said. "Would you look into the death of Mildred Pilsudski?"

Eight

❖

ydia Hopkins looked serene when she came through
the door to take a chair on the opposite side of the
table. Their reached hands touched.

"Hello, Sister Kimberly. How are Joyce and Emtee
Dempsey?"

"Joyce is downstairs. Only one of us could come up."

"I know."

"We are more determined than ever to prove your innocence."

"We?"

"Yes."

"Don't bother. You heard me say I did it."

"Yes, I heard you. I don't believe it."

Lydia shrugged. "I'm grateful, but don't waste your
time, Sister."

"There is someone you are protecting."

Lydia's expression was that of a woman who had already
said good-bye to freedom and found the ways of the out-

side world strange. Kim had the feeling she was being observed from some point in outer space, although her fingers still touched Lydia's.

"I talked to Beverly John."

It took time for the name to penetrate and then Lydia looked genuinely surprised. "How on earth did you ever find out about her?"

"William Dunning told me how to find her."

"Bill! But he knew nothing at all about that. I never told him."

Kim thought about it. "I don't know when he learned of GEM Services. But he had to pay their bill."

"He did not! I paid her."

Kim did not yet understand what she had stumbled into, but her years with Emtee Dempsey suggested caution.

"Where did you first hear of Beverly John?"

"If she presented another statement, Bill should not have paid it." The little flurry of emotion gave way to calm. "She didn't seem like someone who would do that, try to get double payment."

"How much did you pay her?"

"Not quite a thousand dollars."

"And that was the end of it?"

"Yes."

Kim left it there, not knowing what point had been reached. Emtee Dempsey would have to decide how to go on from there.

"I had a nice talk with Mr. Fenwick."

"Oh?" Lydia seemed wary.

"Emtee Dempsey wanted to know more about how your golf clubs got into his garage."

"Is she satisfied?"

"Yes. He would like to come see you."

"No! I don't want him to see me here. He'll understand." Lydia turned her hand over and studied her life

138

line. Her eyes lifted to Kim's. "You spoke with Beverly John?"

"Yes."

"Tell me about it."

Kim would have liked to take a recess and talk to Emtee Dempsey, if only on the phone. She did not understand what Lydia had said about Beverly John, or her claim to have paid GEM Services' bill. It made no sense that she would have paid the person her husband had hired to follow her. Besides, Beverly John said William Dunning had paid her bill. Yet Lydia claimed to have paid almost one thousand dollars.

"You paid her nearly a thousand dollars?"

"Yes."

"Was it worth it?"

A sad smile came over Lydia's face. "No. No, on balance I don't think so."

"Did you expect her to find out something about your husband?"

"My husband!" Lydia tried to laugh, but could not bring it off. She sat sideways in her chair, as if she wanted to go back to her cell. The only course open to Kim was to put the questions Emtee Dempsey wanted answered.

"How often did you golf?"

"As seldom as possible."

"How often is that?"

"I doubt I went out six times a year toward the end. I was in the Women's Monday League when I first started to play. Nine holes on Monday mornings. But it was too confining. If I didn't want to go, I had to get a substitute. Besides, some of the women took it very seriously and I couldn't. I was never very good at it."

"Where were your clubs kept?"

"In my locker."

"Where many people could have got hold of them?"

"But none who had any reason to kill . . ." She couldn't say it. *To kill my husband and daughter.* Kim did not blame her. But if Lydia could not say the words, how could she perform the deed?

"Where did you last see your clubs?"

Her eyes lifted so that she was looking over Kim's head. "In the pro shop, when I left them there for cleaning."

"When was that?"

"After the murders."

Not only did Lydia say the word, her eyes now met Kim's in a lifeless expression. "I knew if I left them there Benny would be sure to clean them. He always had before."

"But not thoroughly enough?"

"Apparently not."

Kim drove home by way of Elmhurst and when she came up the drive of the Elm Stand Town & Country Club, it was difficult to believe that only a week before she had come here to interview Jane Flannery, Fritz, and Phyllis. She didn't want to see any of them again. They would find Lydia's confession only an unsurprising, if long overdue, admission of guilt. She parked the VW in a lot to the side of the clubhouse and took a walk flanked by a boxwood hedge to the pro shop. The door was open and she hesitated but then went on in. After all, it was a store.

Joyce would have loved it. There was clothing, of course, lots of it: shoes and sweaters and caps and hats and jackets, both windbreakers and blazers, and socks. And golfing gloves. In one corner were the clubs. There were sets of irons, sets of woods, there were racks holding such special clubs as wedges, sand wedges, and putters. The putters ran from simple blades to shapes that looked like rejected pieces of an ill-designed machine. Kim took from the rack one of the more complicated putters and was sur-

140

prised by its weight. She settled it on the carpet and wondered how anyone could miss the hole with this. She looked down the shaft at a convergence of white lines on the gray metal that formed an arrow that should have made lining up a putt almost automatic.

"You wanna try it, go ahead."

He had the body of a man but the face of a child. His eyes seemed to look out at her from some bower in the Garden of Eden. Prelapsarian, innocent.

"Where?"

"The practice green."

"I'll need a ball."

He turned and went to the counter, his walk the careening progress of a child, yet somehow agile, and took from a display bowl a lemon-colored ball. His expression was solemn as he handed it to Kim.

"Are you Benny?"

"I don't know you."

"I've only been here once before."

A frown darkened his brow. "Aren't you a member?"

"No."

"A guest?" His tone was hopeful.

Kim shook her head.

He held out his hand. He wanted the ball back. Despite the man's simple manner, Kim might have asked him some questions, but before she could, a short, leathery-skinned man with too-white teeth came in, a study in plaid and insincerity.

"Can I help you, dear lady?"

"I'm looking for Mr. Byron."

"You have found him." His mouth stretched and his teeth gleamed. "Has Benny been trying to sell you a putter?"

"He was being very kind."

"Of course he was. Better get back to work, Benny," he

said to the childlike man, and Benny drifted away among the racks and through a door and was gone. Byron turned to Kim. "I don't believe we've met."

"My name is Kimberly Moriarity. Lydia Hopkins stayed at our house after she was released from prison."

"I thought she was living with some nuns."

"That's right."

The smile seemed frozen now and his small brown eyes darted about as he looked at her in a far different way. "Are you . . ."

"A nun? Yes, I am."

He was actually embarrassed. "And what would you want to see me about?"

"Lydia's golf clubs, of course. As I understand it, they were here in the pro shop when you were hired to replace Mr. Fenwick."

"Whoa," he said, regaining control over his smile. "Wait a moment, now. Whoever told you that was saying more than I think anyone knows for sure. Except Mrs. Hopkins, of course. Apparently her clubs were here in the pro shop, out back, among the clubs waiting to be cleaned and the like. But how long they had been there, I just wouldn't want to say."

"But you did send them to Fenwick?"

"What I did was send along to him a number of things that seemed to me at the time to belong to him or in any case to be his responsibility, not mine."

"Including Lydia Hopkins's golf clubs?"

"As it turns out, as it turns out. But if you were to ask me, did I send Lydia Hopkins's golf clubs to Fenwick, I would have to say, yes and no. That I did is sure, but that I meant to do it is another thing. My point is, I didn't know they were her clubs when I sent them to Fenwick."

"Then why were they sent to him?"

His smile drove the corners of his mouth out of sight. "If it wasn't done intentionally, there is no why to look for."

"How did they get from here to Fenwick's?"

"In a golf cart. Benny wanted to use that damned motor scooter of his, but I persuaded him he didn't want to take twenty trips. He did it in two. Adam lives in one of the condos along the sixteenth fairway. No problem. Not until Adam realized he had Lydia's clubs and decided to call a press conference, that is."

"Her clubs were here in the pro shop during the trial, when the prosecutor was making a point of her clubs not being in her locker?"

"That's the way it looks."

"They must have searched the clubhouse when her clubs were not in her locker."

"They did."

"And it never occurred to anyone that the clubs might be somewhere else, in the pro shop?"

"Don't ask me. It doesn't make a hell of a lot of sense. They should have found them. Maybe they were too eager to think she had gotten rid of them."

"That would have been William Dunning's responsibility, not the prosecutor's," Emtee Dempsey said.

Katherine cleared her throat. "Or Lydia's. Surely she should have told her lawyer what she had done with her clubs."

"Told him that after she had used them to strike her husband she then drove to the club, dropped them off at the pro shop, and went on to her lawyer's?"

"What are you suggesting?"

"That we take our cue from Mr. Byron and regard with skepticism the claim that Lydia's golf clubs have been lan-

143

guishing in the pro shop for years and then were carted up the road to Mr. Fenwick's garage."

Kim wished she did not feel they were returning to idle speculation about what had or had not happened.

"Sister Kimberly," Emtee Dempsey said, "as I understand your conversation with him, Mr. Fenwick spoke of discovering Lydia's clubs among the things that had been brought to his garage from the pro shop. But he did not say that when these things arrived, Lydia's clubs were among them. Nor of course did he deny it. The truth is, I suspect, that he does not know one way or the other if her clubs were among the items originally brought from the pro shop. They could have been put into the garage among those other things at a later time."

"You must be sure to convey those thoughts to Mr. Dunning, Sister," Katherine said. "Clearly those clubs will play a major role in the coming trial."

Sister Mary Teresa frowned, but apparently not because of Katherine's gloomy concession that another trial would actually be convened, despite Emtee Dempsey's resolution to identify the true murderer and render a new trial unnecessary—at least one in which Lydia was the defendant.

"I would like to speak to Mr. Dunning about the death of Mildred Pilsudski. Do bring Sister Kimberly up to date on that, Katherine."

"I wish I thought it could help Lydia," Katherine said, her tone gloomier still. "In any case, I won't begin until someone brings me at least a glass of wine."

Katherine had two glasses of wine in the course of reporting, first, that the verdict of suicide was a preliminary one that was being vigorously contested by Mildred Pilsudski's children and, second, that William Dunning had interviewed the GEM Services employee the day before her death.

"Which is why," Emtee Dempsey said to Kim, "I already asked him to stop by tonight. I would have been prompted to do so by what you have said, Sister, but now we have multiple reasons for wanting to talk with him."

"You just asked him to stop by?"

"I told him I knew things he should know."

Katherine said, "He won't come. May I go on?"

The coroner's initial finding was reasonable enough. A sixty-one-year-old woman had been found behind the wheel of her car, in her closed garage, with the motor still running, dead. There were no signs of a struggle. It looked like dozens of other suicides he had seen. Nor was he particularly surprised when the family, a Polish Catholic family, horrified by the implications of their mother propelling herself into the next world by her own hand, raised the roof about the verdict. That too was common.

"But theirs is not simply a general complaint. One daughter had spoken to her mother an hour before she was found in the garage, asking her help with something she was baking, and the mother had offered to come over and show her how to make the pastry. It seemed obvious that she had gone into the garage, started her car, and then had trouble with the remote control that opened the door. Before she could get it to work properly, the fumes had begun to affect her. Doctor Wrenkley is almost certain to reverse his verdict."

"To natural death," Emtee Dempsey said. "Replacing one error with another."

Katherine looked at Kim. "Our dear friend insists that this too was death by violence."

"How do you know that she had seen William Dunning the day before?"

"Her datebook that Wrenkley kindly let me examine, along with the other items in her purse. She met him at four-thirty the previous day."

"At his office?"

"At Wimpy's in Oak Park."

"Did you check with Beverly John to see what the point of the meeting was?"

Emtee Dempsey nodded. "That is something you must do, Sister Kimberly. No matter what we may be told by William Dunning."

But they were to be told nothing by William Dunning. He did not come to the house on Walton Street and when, at 10:30, Kim telephoned his apartment, at Emtee Dempsey's insistence, the phone was answered by a recording device that invited her to leave a message. She didn't accept the invitation. She hated answering machines.

"Nonsense," Sister Mary Teresa said. "Call it again and leave this message."

She actually wrote it out, in block letters, and handed it to Kim. Kim dialed, listened again to the recorded invitation, and at the sound of the buzzer read what the old nun had written.

"'When you come see me please bring the reports you were given by GEM Services.'"

"Beverly John kept copies," Kim said, after she hung up.

"We may want to see those after Mr. Dunning lets us see what he has. You needn't mention this when you see her tomorrow."

The two old friends had listened with interest to Kim's account of her talk with Lydia Hopkins, and Kim knew the old nun had been puzzling over the significance of Lydia's claim to have paid GEM Services nearly one thousand dollars. Katherine said she did not intend to leave until she heard what Emtee Dempsey made of this attempt at double payment.

"I think the explanation is obvious."

"What is the explanation?"

"As Sister Kimberly surmised in questioning Lydia, she

146

and Jeffrey had both and independently hired the same agency. Any ethical violation that exists might lie there."

Katherine was not receptive. "Surely that would be too great a coincidence. You can't mean that they knowingly hired the same agency. The chances of their doing it unwittingly seem slim indeed."

"One more question to put to William Dunning," Sister Mary Teresa said grimly. "I must confess to being very annoyed at his attempt to duck these questions."

Later, lying awake in her bed, Kim wondered why William Dunning should ever answer Emtee Dempsey's summons. Whatever leverage the old nun had had with the lawyer was provided by Lydia Hopkins, but now Lydia had confessed to the murders of her husband and daughter. Dunning no longer needed the house on Walton Street in which to conceal his client and it seemed unlikely that Lydia would be inclined to persuade her lawyer to go to Emtee Dempsey. The only support the old nun had outside this house came from Katherine Senski.

In the still of the night with the murmur of the incessant traffic on Walton Street lifting to her, Kim could not remember what it had been that weakened her conviction that Emtee Dempsey was heading for humiliation. She had promised to prove that Lydia Hopkins was innocent and everything went against that even before Lydia had publicly announced that she was indeed guilty. Rather than be floored by this turn of events, Emtee Dempsey had taken it as vindication. Lydia had confessed to protect the real murderer. But until a real murderer was found this only compounded the old nun's predicament. Not that her earlier cockiness would have been forgotten if she had chosen silence after Lydia's confession.

Richard Monday had alluded to her promise that she would prove Lydia innocent, and although he had not named Sister Mary Teresa the reporters there would have known to whom he referred. Richard predictably was less subtle but thank God he was also less public.

"Is she going to call us all together and admit her mistake?" he asked Kim on the phone.

"Mistake?"

"Bluff. Brag. Promise. Call it what you want. You do remember her saying she would prove Lydia Hopkins was innocent."

"I hardly need to *remember* it. She continues to say the same thing."

"Kim, for crying out loud, call her off. I have had my differences with the old girl, but I don't want to see her get any more hurt than she already is. Monday is in hog heaven right now. Lydia Hopkins did his work for him. He has triumphed over Carrillo without lifting a finger. You heard him with those reporters. If he finds out she's still promising to blow his case out of the water, he could very well subpoena her and ask her what she knows."

"I'll tell her."

"Call it friendly advice."

It was the last thing Kim had said to Sister Mary Teresa before they went to the chapel for night prayers. Katherine had gone off in a cab, Joyce was still listening to a ball game on the television in the basement apartment.

"I accept it as friendly advice."

"You're not giving up?"

"Certainly not. Richard could very well be right about how it will end. I had thought a trial could be prevented, but he is right, that may very well be the way to expose the murderer."

"Who do you think it is?"

The old nun smiled, but only for a moment. She put a hand on Kim's arm. "The awful thing about delaying is the danger. There could be more deaths and already there have been four."

"Sister, who is it?"

She wagged a pudgy finger. "Not tonight. But you can sleep easily nonetheless. There is no longer any doubt of Lydia's innocence."

Kim just looked at the old nun, fearing a direct question would invite another teasing postponement.

"Sister Kimberly, not even Lydia can claim to have killed Mildred Pilsudski."

Emtee Dempsey then bustled into the chapel, and throughout the recitation of the evening prayer Kim had known a sense of peace not completely derived from the Psalms they recited.

But now in bed she could not ignore the many assumptions of Emtee Dempsey's confident remark. If the deaths of Jeffrey and Laura Hopkins, as well as of Dolores Merrill and Mildred Pilsudski, were brought about by the same person, then indeed Lydia was innocent since she was behind bars in the county jail when Mildred Pilsudski had died. But had the woman been murdered? And what connection did her death have to the others? To assume that whoever had killed Dolores Merrill had killed Jeffrey and Laura was already to go far beyond anything they knew. Fenwick's theory that someone had come in off the sixteenth fairway and done the deed out of vicious irrationality was at least as plausible.

The Japanese restaurant to which William Dunning took her after calling for her on Monday at the house on Walton Street, prompting Joyce to make jokes about her date, was a novelty for Kim, and a revelation. The waitresses wore kimonos; there was a knee-high fountain in the lobby, a block of granite in whose scooped-out top lay three pebbles bathed in a constant flow of water. Simple. Soothing.

Their table was next to a floor-to-ceiling window

149

through which they had a view of a miniature garden in which a miniature stream flowed. It was difficult to believe that this restaurant was in the heart of Chicago.

Ordering the food and then eating it with chopsticks so absorbed them that it was not until the dishes had been cleared away and they had bowls of green-tea ice cream that they got around to the reason Kim had asked the lawyer if they might meet.

"So long as it's not in my office," he had said, hence this Japanese restaurant. Now he explained that every available surface in his office was covered with materials needed for Lydia's defense.

"You said you paid GEM Services money owed them because of what they had done for Jeffrey Hopkins."

"For following his wife, to be exact. I can't tell you how reluctant I was to honor that bill."

"Lydia says she paid GEM nearly a thousand dollars."

"When?"

"Before she went to prison."

"It would have had to be. I have been handling her finances ever since."

"Do you know a Mrs. Mildred Pilsudski?"

"Aha." He sat back in his chair. "So that's what you want to know."

"You do know her."

He leaned forward, his arms on the table. "How does it work? You go out and try to lure flies into the web while Sister Mary Teresa sits patiently in the center of it waiting to devour her victims?"

"I report to her what I learn."

"Sister, let me say a few words directly to you. I know you admire Sister Mary Teresa. I admire her. Everyone does. Equally, I have no doubt that she wants very much to help Lydia. How can I persuade her that the best thing she can do for Lydia is stop sending you around making these inquiries?"

"She is convinced Lydia is innocent."

"Is she? Well, I have pleaded her not guilty in a courtroom and if her innocence is defended it will be there, not in a convent study. And the way it will be defended is with evidence and facts, not by intuition and someone being for whatever reason certain she is innocent."

"Don't you think she is innocent?"

"My professional reputation is engaged in the effort to prove she is not guilty." He looked out the window and sighed. The little stream went under a little bridge. The scene was suggestive of an unreal peace.

"Do you think you will succeed?"

"Don't expect me to promise I will. That sort of stunt I will leave to Sister Mary Teresa. What disappoints me is that she doesn't seem to have considered that Monday will very likely take a deposition and ask her what basis she has for asserting the innocence of Lydia Hopkins. If she has none, she will be ridiculed. Think what that will do for his case. Not even the great Mary Teresa Dempsey can show Lydia to be innocent. The defense would never recover from that."

"It isn't simply intuition."

"If she knows something I think she should tell me about it."

"She is certain that whoever killed Mrs. Pilsudski, also—"

"Killed!" He did not unclench his teeth as he said the word. "She killed herself."

"Is that verdict certain?"

"Because the family contests it? Five times out of ten

rulings of suicide are contested by the family. The verdict is almost never reversed."

"The coroner himself sounds doubtful."

"You've talked with the coroner?"

"No. But Sister Mary Teresa received the information from a source she could not possibly doubt."

His smile was not happy. "One way or the other, it doesn't make a damned bit of difference so far as Lydia's trial is concerned."

"Of course it does. Obviously, Lydia could not have killed Mrs. Pilsudski. Lydia was in jail at the time."

"I am sure that Monday would be delighted to concede she didn't kill Mrs. Pilsudski, particularly since the woman committed suicide. Lydia is not on trial for that."

"But, if the person who killed Mrs. Pilsudski also killed Dolores Merrill and—"

"Stop!" He said it again, with a smile and in a lowered tone. "Please, stop. She is going to have to cut out this kind of wild speculation. There is no connection between Dolores Merrill and the deaths of Jeffrey and Laura Hopkins. As for Mildred Pilsudski . . ." He threw up his hands in a helpless gesture.

"Did Mrs. Pilsudski work for you?"

"No."

"She worked for GEM Services."

"So I understand."

"Did you ever hire GEM Services?"

"Beverly John did some odds and ends for me years ago. That's why I had her address and phone number on file. That had nothing to do with Mrs. Pilsudski."

"Why did you meet with her?"

"Did I meet with her?"

"That's what we were told."

Kim hoped that her voice and expression did not betray how tenuous Sister Mary Teresa's conjectures sounded bouncing off the skepticism of William Dunning. His threat that Emtee Dempsey would be exposed filled Kim with dread. It was all too plausible. Earlier she had wished that it were Joyce rather than herself who was here enjoying this Japanese restaurant. She herself had little luck in identifying what it was that was put before her, but Joyce would have wanted to learn to prepare such dishes. Now for cowardly reasons she wished Joyce were here. Was it really possible that Emtee Dempsey's long-applauded knack for seeing what others didn't see had deserted her at last? Kim had little doubt that it would require a defeat as resounding as this promised to be to convince the old nun that her day was over.

"What will you tell her, Sister?"

"What you have told me."

"All of it?"

"Certainly."

"And you will urge her to help Lydia Hopkins by stopping her efforts to help her?"

"It wouldn't do any good."

"Not even if her way of helping Lydia could actually harm her?"

"She would never intentionally harm anyone."

"Bully for her."

"Why don't you talk to me about Mrs. Pilsudski? Sister Mary Teresa will learn the truth sooner or later."

"I rejoice for her. I have neither truth nor falsehoods to offer her."

In the lobby the three stones in the indentation of the knee-high pillar were still being bathed in water. Perhaps the water flowed forever. How long would it be before it eroded the stones? The three stones might have been the remnant of the Order of Martha and Mary living on Walton Street. The largest would be Emtee Dempsey. Kim wished she could retain as unwavering a grasp on the notion of Lydia's innocence as even her lawyer.

"He is paid for it," she told herself, but it was not a consoling remark.

By and large, Beverly John showed professional poise when she came to the house on Walton Street in answer to Sister Mary Teresa Dempsey's invitation, although when Kim first opened the door, she thought the president of GEM Services' posture was ramrod stiff and the smile on her face a conscious effort.

"It was good of you to come," Kim said.

"It was good of you to set it up so soon. I feel like a fan granted an interview with a star. I don't know what in the world I'll say to her."

"Then just let her do the talking," Kim said, hoping she wasn't audible in the kitchen. She didn't want sarcastic laughter from Joyce to mar the occasion.

In the study, Beverly John began to gush—it didn't seem too strong a word—her admiration for Sister Mary Teresa. She wanted the old nun to know that she had given hope to a lot of women caught in a man's world.

"Nonsense," the old nun said, cutting her off. "It is I who admires you. What I have heard of your organization only makes me want to hear more. Will you have coffee or tea?"

"Coffee is made," Kim said, remembering the viscous brew she had been served in Beverly John's office.

"I think I would like tea," the investigator said, and it might have been a bid for upward social mobility.

"Tea it is," Kim said. "Sister?"

"Tea sounds just right."

When Kim left the study, Beverly John was settled into a chair across from Emtee Dempsey's desk. The old nun, hands folded on the blotter, beamed at her guest. "A woman detective," she was saying as Kim closed the door.

Joyce, who had not been told of the visit, was as impressed as Emtee Dempsey.

"Why don't you bring the tea and then stay?" Kim suggested.

This had the added advantage of getting Kim more quickly back to the study, where an enthralled Emtee Dempsey was listening to a somewhat diffidently stated account of the genesis of GEM Services. Beverly John had worked in a minor post in the adjutant general's office when she was a WAAC and, after her discharge, for an investigative office of state government.

"But never actually as a policewoman?"

"No."

"How exactly does one become a private investigator?"

Beverly John, flattered now, gave a detailed account of the way she had gotten her license, floated a loan to start her agency, survived a lean year or two, but now had three full-time employees and others she used on special assignments.

"Into which category would Mrs. Pilsudski fall?"

"Poor Mildred. She had been full-time, but for the past few months had been willing to take only single assignments and ones that weren't likely to go on and on."

"She was doing something for William Dunning?"

"Not as my employee."

"Then how did you know she was seeing him? You were the source of that information, were you not?"

Beverly John nodded. Her manner now was as it had been when Kim visited her in the office of GEM Services. She seemed to be waiting for the right question to be asked.

"Had you ever done any work for William Dunning?"

155

"Yes."

"You mean the money he paid you for what you had done for Jeffrey?"

"Assuming that, since he had the power of attorney and could pay me and that he received the reports, I worked for him."

"Lydia Hopkins says she paid you nearly a thousand dollars."

Beverly John sat forward more tensely, looking across the desk at Emtee Dempsey. "She did."

"And Mr. Dunning paid you the remainder of the fee." Beverly John was silent for a moment, then shook her head. "That is not accurate. Lydia paid me in full."

"They each hired you, didn't they?" Kim asked. It was like winning at charades. Beverly John rewarded her with a smile.

"That's right."

"And why did Lydia hire you?"

"All inquiries are confidential, Sister Mary Teresa."

"I understand that. And you would keep Lydia's confidence because you feel obliged to and what obliges you is the well-being of the client. Am I right?"

"I promise that I will and I keep my promises."

Emtee Dempsey nodded. "Let me put you a case. A person comes and hires your services for a purpose we will designate as X. You agree to keep X a confidential matter because doing so best serves your client. Imagine now that by keeping that promise you bring harm to the client. What is your obligation then?"

"Well, if I made a promise . . ."

"You've made a promise," Emtee Dempsey agreed patiently, "and we have spelled out the purpose for which the promise is made. But if that purpose is thwarted rather than served by keeping the promise, your obligation to keep the promise is removed, is it not?"

156

Beverly John obviously found this reasoning both persuasive and repellent.

"What good is a promise then?"

"It is as good as the reason for making it. You may justifiably break the promise if the original point of making it is thereby served. I assure you that this is sound doctrine."

"You want me to tell you why Lydia Hopkins hired me?"

"Because I think it will help me in my effort to prove her innocent and thus save her from a lifetime in prison. Would you want to visit her after her trial in prison and assure her that you had kept your promise to her even if it had the unhappy consequence of putting her in that cell?"

"She could absolve me from the promise!"

"That's true. And we would waste valuable time, days perhaps, asking her to do so."

Kim admired Beverly John's reluctance even as she grew impatient with it. But if Beverly John was reluctant, Emtee Dempsey was persistent; it was an unequal struggle and soon, in the best interests of Lydia Hopkins, Beverly John was divulging the investigation she had undertaken for her and for which she had received not quite one thousand dollars.

"Is that a high fee?"

"It could have been infinitely high. Lost persons are often lost for good so far as those who want to find them are concerned. But we had some lucky breaks and managed to locate the woman."

"And who precisely is she?"

"Not is. Was. There really wasn't that much distinctive about her. She had been a librarian in Rochester, Minnesota, for the last fifteen years of her life. Apparently her health was bad and she had moved there to be close to the Mayo Clinic."

"Was she treated there?"

"Their records were decisive in finding her. But she had not been to the clinic for years. She died in her bed of a massive heart attack."

"Was it her heart that brought her to Rochester?"

"Maybe her broken heart."

"How do you mean?"

"Her physical ailment was a species of cancer that underwent remission after remission. And in the end it was her heart that did her in."

"Her broken heart. She was single?"

"Yes, but she had a baby in Atlanta."

"Ah."

Kim said, "Did you find out who the child is?"

"Mrs. Hopkins stopped the investigation after we found the woman."

"What was the woman's name?"

"Sarah. Sarah Jones."

"Jones?"

"She changed her name when she went to Minnesota; not legally, she just started calling herself Sarah Jones. That would have made it impossible to trace her if she had not contacted the clinic before coming to Rochester. Under her real name, Sarah Rooney. When we checked out Sarah Rooney we were told that she was still in town. Our informant assumed she had married someone named Jones."

Sister Mary Teresa stared hard at Beverly John. "Who do you think that woman was?"

"I don't know."

"Why did Lydia Hopkins want to find her?"

Beverly looked at Kim, then back to Emtee Dempsey. "She said that if we found out it could be a present for a friend of hers."

"A present?"

"Letting him know what had happened to Sarah Rooney."

"Did she say who that friend was?"

"A Mr. Fenwick."

The old nun exchanged a glance with Kim, and Kim knew what she was thinking, but they were in the process of extracting information from, not giving information to, Beverly John.

"Let us return now to the unfortunate Mrs. Pilsudski." Emtee Dempsey said. "Mildred Pilsudski worked for you, you had worked for William Dunning, Mildred Pilsudski was in contact with Mr. Dunning, yet you say she was not working for you."

"He wanted her to work for him."

"Conduct an investigation for him?"

"He wanted a copy of the report on the investigation we had conducted for Mrs. Hopkins."

"And he contacted Mrs. Pilsudski rather than you?"

"He knew I wouldn't let him have them." She looked suddenly sad. "Unless he could have talked me around like you did."

"Cooperating with me and cooperating with William Dunning are, I assure you, quite different things. Did Mrs. Pilsudski come to you with this story?"

"Not exactly. I found her rummaging through my files and she burst out with the whole story almost immediately. When she told me what he had offered her, I found it difficult to blame her."

"How much?"

"One thousand dollars."

"He wanted the report very badly."

"Well, he didn't get the whole thing."

"How did he get any?"

"I permitted Mrs. Pilsudski to tell him all but the identi-

159

fication of the woman. It seemed a shame to let a thousand dollars slip away."

The old nun hummed. "Did she get the thousand dollars?"

"Yes. And gave me the half I insisted on."

"Ah. Do you suppose he realized he had not been given the full report?"

Beverly John sat for a moment in silence. "I don't know."

"What were your first thoughts when you learned of the death of Mrs. Pilsudski?"

A wry smile played on her thin lips. "I thought that five hundred dollars hadn't been worth it after all and I wondered who would end up with it."

Emtee Dempsey seemed about to say more but thought better of it. Beverly John refused more tea, the visit ended, and, after Kim had shown the investigator to the door, she returned to the study.

"Sarah."

"Yes," Kim replied.

"I think I would like to have a talk with Mr. Fenwick, Sister. Do you think you can arrange that?"

"Right away."

Nine

F enwick proved remarkably reluctant to come to the house on Walton Street and a day elapsed before Kim made the arrangements. These included going for Fenwick since he no longer drove ("Except on the golf course, where I drive both ball and cart") and was wary of taxis for reasons he was all too willing to elaborate on. Kim sat smiling through anecdotes about overcharges in St. Louis and Boston and an adventure in Pasadena in the middle of a traffic jam that had cost him an interview that might have led to a life in California.

Fenwick smiled. "California still seemed on the other side of the moon in those days. This was before the war— the Second World War. After the war, I was more than happy to be a club pro. The prize money on the tour was far from what it has become and travel was horrendous. Settling down here in Elmhurst seemed to be the reason we had fought the war."

Kim accepted the offer of a car from Mr. Rush, not

wanting to show up at Fenwick's door in the battered VW. His golf cart seemed as much designed for public roads as their VW. Mr. Rush's car came with a driver.

"Good old Mr. Rush," Joyce said admiringly, looking out at the magnificent vehicle parked at their curb.

"Timothy has infallible taste in all things," Emtee Dempsey said infallibly.

"Why don't you come along, Joyce?"

"No, thanks. I have brownies in the oven and the Cubs on the tube."

Joyce went back to her kitchen, Emtee Dempsey to her study, and Kim was taken in a very long automobile of gun-metal gray to the Elm Stand Town & Country Club. There was a bar and television in the backseat of the car. On the set was the news and Kim listened to an interview on the courthouse steps with Prosecutor Monday. A man who a few weeks before had appeared before the cameras wearing the look of defeat and shame now fairly exuded the confidence of the victor. He had reached such heights of confidence that he could afford a species of magnanimity, although Carrillo would have called it by a different name.

"I think every citizen can sympathize with Lydia Hopkins, who has been put through an ordeal worthy of Dostoyevsky because of the incompetence of public officials."

"You mean Judge Marsha Hunt?"

"No!" Alarm was bright in the prosecutor's eyes. Insulting judges was no way to reach his ends. "I mean my predecessors in this office. Judge Hunt was perfectly right in making the judgment she made. You will notice that the full court let it stand. The judges thus agree that there were serious flaws in the previous trial. There will be no flaws in this one."

"Because she admitted her guilt?" a reporter asked.

162

"She is pleading not guilty as before."

"But isn't that just a legal stratagem?"

"The courtroom is the stage on which legal stratagems, as you put it, are played out. It is society's way. . . ."

Kim turned off the set. The driver nodded as if in agreement. Did he too think Lydia innocent? If so, he had learned to think so from Timothy Rush. Kim tried to derive consolation from the thought that if a lawyer of Mr. Rush's experience thought Lydia had a chance, it might well be that William Dunning could bring her through. Hadn't Emtee Dempsey said that Mr. Rush was infallible? Unfortunately, it was the old nun's infallibility that was on the line.

The thought that Lydia's fate depended on William Dunning bothered Kim and she sat in the center of the plush backseat of Mr. Rush's car, staring straight ahead, invisible behind the opaque windows of the car, thinking of Lydia's lawyer.

Fenwick had said the lawyer was half in love with Lydia, however subconsciously, but it was hard to interpret the lawyer's actions as helpful to his client's cause. His desire that Sister Mary Teresa drop her interest in Lydia's fate had a superficial justification, but in the light of his own odd behavior in the case of Mrs. Pilsudski, it was hard to think of him as a friend of Lydia's.

"All he had to do is ask for a subpoena instructing Beverly John to turn over the report as relevant to the trail. There was no need to attempt to buy it unless he wished to keep what he was doing secret."

Emtee Dempsey had spoken these words in measured tones after Beverly John had left the house on Walton Street. Kim couldn't bring herself to formulate the question that surged up in her, but Joyce didn't hesitate to ask it.

"Do you think William Dunning killed Mrs. Pilsudski?"

"I seem to be the only one who thinks she was killed."

"If she was?"

Emtee Dempsey turned to Kim, her eyes still bright despite the hour. "Some would say I have made too many judgments and promises as it is."

Upstairs in her room Kim had considered the implications of Dunning as killer of Mrs. Pilsudski. Emtee Dempsey seemed to be working on the assumption that the four deaths were the work of one murderer. Just imagine a trial in which the defense lawyer was himself the guilty party and permitted his client to go to prison for the deed he had performed!

Nothing Kim knew of Mr. Dunning made that plausible. No wonder Richard and others objected to Emtee Dempsey sitting behind her desk in her study on Walton Street, weaving intricate explanations of events that were for the most part only algebraic symbols for her, abstract events. True, she knew Lydia and she had spoken with Dunning several times, but seeing people in the house on Walton Street was not the same as seeing them in their native habitats. Thank God nonetheless that she was bringing Mr. Fenwick to Emtee Dempsey. The golf pro was only a talking head on television for the old nun.

The car had been passed through the gate of the Elm Stand Town & Country Club and was now sweeping up the drive. This seemed to be the appropriate way to approach that elegant clubhouse, in the backseat of what once would have been called a limousine. Kim directed the driver around the house, between the tennis courts and pool, and on around the practice putting green to the road that wound through great beeches and walnuts to the condominiums along the sixteenth fairway. This was the road on which Benny would have driven the golf cart laden with things from the pro shop. Ahead on the road,

164

resplendent in blue blazer, yellow shirt, and knit maroon tie, stood Adam Fenwick. Kim was sure that Emtee Dempsey would have pronounced him a fine figure of a man.

The driver stopped and hurried around to open the door for Fenwick. The elegant elderly man paused before getting in, his face registering surprise.

"If I had known about this, I would have taken the vow of poverty myself."

"It's not ours."

He retained her hand after the initial greeting and whispered to Kim, "I feel I am being summoned to the principal's office."

"Just admit your guilt and the punishment will be minimal."

"I am afraid my guilts are not fit for convent walls."

He became fascinated with the car then. Kim turned on the television but could find only soaps. It didn't matter; Fenwick had discovered the bar. He was impressed that it had a sink with running water.

"Well, why not?" he said. "Boats and planes have had them for years. Can I fix you a drink, Sister?"

"No, but you go ahead."

"Softening me up for the grilling?"

He took ice from the diminutive refrigerator and poured half an ounce of bourbon over the cubes, then added water. "Cheers."

Kim nodded. Fenwick's nervousness was obviously not feigned.

However she did it, Sister Mary Teresa had Fenwick at his ease within five minutes of his arrival at the house on Walton Street. He certainly would not have found her greeting a threat.

"Mr. Fenwick, I have wanted for so long a time to thank

165

you personally for your noble efforts to help our mutual friend, Lydia Hopkins. How few of those who knew her have risen to her defense."

"I seem to have landed her in worse trouble."

"That I strongly doubt. On the contrary. You precipitated events that will lead to the complete exoneration of Lydia Hopkins."

The old nun stopped in the hallway and faced Fenwick as she spoke these words, then she continued on to the study. Kim winced at this ringing renewal of confidence. Nor was Emtee Dempsey simply relying on the system doing its job. Inside the study, she led Fenwick to the chair opposite her desk.

"And, Mr. Fenwick, I have publicly stated and now solemnly repeat that I shall show her to be innocent."

As soon as she got behind the desk the conversation centered on golf and Fenwick's lifelong involvement in it. Emtee Dempsey listened with the rapture of a student and Fenwick was happy to play instructor to this legendary intellectual. Kim listened to him describe the origin of the game, the quaint names once given the various clubs, the emergence of the standard modern set. Emtee Dempsey nodded with interest while he explained that the higher the number of the club, the less distance it was good for.

"I find it hard to imagine Lydia carrying around that many clubs."

Fenwick explained about golf bags and carts and was now thoroughly at his ease, aided in part by the bourbon and water Kim put in his hand. Why did she feel they were shanghaiing this dapper man?

"Are you a native of Chicago, Mr. Fenwick?"

"Please call me Adam. No. I came here after World War Two, a long time ago certainly, but prior to that I had been a kind of nomad, as many professional golfers are. I settled here and there for lengths of time, but then I would move on."

"What is your native city?"

"Minneapolis. A good place for a golfer to move from, of course; the season there isn't long enough."

"What are the other cities you spent time in?" Emtee Dempsey asked. "I ask because it sounds so exciting to someone like myself who has been anchored to Chicago all her life."

Fenwick sat back and seemed to read the cities off the study ceiling. Kansas City, St. Louis, Miami, Biloxi, New Orleans, then back east again to Charlotte.

"But you have been here in Chicago for over forty years?"

"That's right." He smiled as if sharing her surprise. "Believe it or not."

"Were you ever in Atlanta?"

Fenwick's eyes lowered to Emtee Dempsey's and the expression of nostalgic joy faded from his face. "Atlanta," he repeated. "Yes, I have lived in Atlanta. During the winter months of 1958." He turned to Kim. "Atlanta is where I met Sarah."

"Sister Kimberly has told me the story. The great lost love of your life."

He nodded. "I was married at the time. I was in Atlanta advising a manufacturer on the promotion of golf clothing. My wife stayed here in Chicago. I met Sarah and fell in love."

A little silence fell and then Fenwick roused himself. "I'm sorry. That episode doesn't concern either of you."

"I wonder," Emtee Dempsey said. "Lydia Hopkins reminded you of Sarah, did she not?"

"There was an uncanny resemblance."

"Did you never speculate why?"

"I don't understand."

167

"If Lydia were related to Sarah, the resemblance would not be so surprising."

"Related?"

"Her daughter. Adam, you knew that, didn't you?"

"Knew Lydia to be Sarah's daughter? Good Lord, no. It never occurred to me." An odd little smile worked at his lips and there was a wondering, awestruck look in his eyes. "*Is* she Sarah's daughter?"

Emtee Dempsey paused. "What do you think?"

Fenwick was all but overcome by a series of emotions. An almost manic smile came and went and when he looked at Kim tears formed in his eyes. "No wonder. I told you how pleasant it was just to sit with her. It was as if thirty years had not passed and I was in Atlanta, enjoying again an unreal relationship with the most wonderful woman I've ever known."

"Relationship," Emtee Dempsey said, managing not to wince at the word. "You and Sarah were intimate?"

The blush rose from Adam Fenwick's collar and soon suffused his face. If he reddened like this with a tanned face, what would he do when pale? He cleared his throat and rattled the diminished ice cubes in his glass. "Yes. I don't know why I'm telling you this. It makes her sound totally different than she was. She thought we would marry. I hadn't told her of my wife and when I did, assuring her that I would immediately obtain a divorce, she was profoundly affected. She knew I had been raised a Catholic and had simply assumed I would not have talked of marriage if I were not truly free. Intimate? Once. Only once. It was on that occasion, afterward, when we were speaking of marriage, that I told her what I thought would preserve our love but which proved to kill it. My promise to get a divorce made me a stranger to her. She had not known I was married. I never saw her again."

168

"Did you ever make an effort to trace her?"

"What good would it have done?"

"Lydia did make that effort. Do you see now who Lydia is?"

If he did, he did not want to be the first to say it, but he leaned expectantly toward Sister Mary Teresa.

"I think Lydia is your daughter, Adam Fenwick. She is the child Sarah conceived with you in Atlanta."

During the ride back to his condominium, Adam Fenwick held Kim's hand tightly in his own, but he said little, lost as he was in a riot of thoughts brought on by the conversation with Sister Mary Teresa. The old nun had made two logical leaps without which her story was a good deal less dramatic. First, that Lydia was the child of Sarah and, second, that the child was conceived in Atlanta, with Adam its father. But these seemed the kinds of fact one could somehow know without knowing them on the basis of documentary evidence. Of course, that evidence would have to be sought and God help them all if it didn't bear out what Emtee Dempsey had said. But Kim herself now thought she knew why Lydia had told Beverly John to stop the investigation.

"I know I'm terrible company just now," Fenwick said, "but this has been a most discombobulating afternoon."

"I can imagine."

"My dear Sister, permit me to doubt that."

Kim laughed. "Did you ever show Lydia a picture of Sarah?"

"Why don't you say 'of her mother'?"

"Did you?"

"I even gave her several. Copies of snapshots I had. She asked for them herself."

Doubtless these had been of help to Beverly John in her investigation.

"I still cannot believe that it never occurred to me even to suspect the relationship. Those photographs were of a Sarah younger than Lydia, but they could have been sisters. I know I said as much. Perhaps I simply didn't want to think about the intervening time because it seemed to me that they were contemporaries."

Before he got out of the car, he said, "You asked the other day if I had visited Lydia. I will do so now, after I have adjusted a bit to this amazing turn of events."

"Will you talk to her of these things?"

"If Sister Mary Teresa is right, Lydia has been way ahead of me on this."

When the car reached the clubhouse, Kim stopped it and told the driver she would no longer need him.

His jaw looked like a padded coat hanger and jutted out further as she spoke.

"Mr. Rush told me to be completely at your disposal."

"You have been and I'm grateful. But I will be staying here some time."

"I'll wait in the parking lot."

"That's not necessary."

He touched his furrowed forehead in a salute and the car glided away. To the parking lot. Kim found it hard to be angry that her car awaited her when she was through speaking with Jane Flannery.

The business manager of the Elm Stand Town & Country Club appeared more managed than managing when Kim looked in. Jane's glance was a helpless one. "It's the GD computer," she cried, and she sounded close to tears.

Two youngish men wearing baseball caps looked over their shoulders, then returned to tinkering with Jane's computer.

"Did you ever have a flat and want to just abandon your

car? Right now I would like to take a hammer to that computer. Who were those people?"

"Luddites."

A great smile broke over Jane's face. "You really are going to turn into another Sister Mary Teresa if you don't watch out."

"All I want is to ask you one question."

"All I want is a cup of coffee. Let's go down to the grill."

They sat at a table near the window and Fritz brought them coffee, indicated that he was glad to see Kim again, and turned to go.

"The computer's out," Jane said to his back.

"I didn't know it was up to bat."

Jane snorted. "If I were Lydia Hopkins I would throw an ashtray at him. Speaking of whom, a lot of water has gone over the dam since we spoke."

"Yes, indeed."

"It must be a relief for her finally to have admitted it."

"Jane, she's protecting someone. She's no more guilty than you or I."

Jane sputtered coffee but managed to get her cup to the table before being convulsed in a coughing fit. When she was done, she looked at Kim with tear-filled eyes. "Tell me I didn't hear what you said."

"Sister Mary Teresa thinks the same thing."

"Sister Mary Teresa is the sweetest, kindest person in the world, but Lydia admits she did it!"

"But why?"

"Because they have the goods on her this time. The golf clubs."

"Isn't it odd that no one found them at the time of the first trial?"

"Is it? They weren't in her locker. They weren't in her

171

home. I suppose they figured they were at the bottom of a lake."

"Or in the golf shop?"

Jane managed another sip of coffee without joking. "Okay. That was dumb. But now they have been found, they link Lydia to the killings, so what can she do? Better to just 'fess up and get it over with."

"Only it isn't that simple. There must be another trial."

"Was that Bill Dunning's fault?"

"If it was a fault."

Jane frowned. "Why prolong it?"

"Maybe he thinks she's innocent."

The corners of Jane's mouth turned down as she tipped her head. "Maybe he's the one protecting someone."

"Isn't that his job as her lawyer?"

"Oh, it's more than that. He never exactly suggested we lie, but when he interviewed those of us who work here, he let us know that if anyone could truly say, for example, that he or she had never seen Lydia golf in years, that would be very helpful. The point being the clubs could have been missing for years. His aim was to show they were unimportant to the case."

"That sounds reasonable enough. Could anyone say that?"

"No." But she stopped herself. "Wait, that's not entirely true. Benny offered to say that. But Benny can hardly be called a reliable witness."

"He looks as if he knows the difference between truth and a lie."

"I suppose. But he liked Lydia. It was because of her that he did the Hopkinses' lawn in summer."

"How did he get there?"

"On his motor scooter. I suppose Benny liked the way she got along so well with Fenwick even though he was retired. They spent a lot of time just talking."

"Where was little Laura then?"

"Around." Had Jane forgotten the picture of the callous, indifferent mother she had painted? Kim asked her that.

"Lydia had her good days. Who doesn't?"

"Jane, I have a very specific question to ask. Do you remember the day of the murders?"

"Of Jeffrey and Laura? I'll never forget it."

"I mean details of it."

"Do you mean what happened at the house?"

"No. I mean what happened here that day."

"You have something particular in mind."

"Did you see William Dunning at the clubhouse that day?"

Jane thought about it for half a minute, squinting out at the practice green. She began to shake her head slowly. "No, I don't remember seeing him."

"You're sure?"

A nod. "Does it matter so much?"

"He was here," another voice said. Fritz spoke from behind the bar. "I heard your question. Sure, Dunning was here that day. He sat at the bar and had three double scotches. Everybody was astounded by what had happened, but it hit him the hardest."

"What time was that?"

"Midafternoon. He sure beat the crowd that day. He came in from the golf shop, and he really looked shell-shocked."

"By midafternoon you mean what? Three o'clock?"

"Later than that. More like four maybe."

Kim was unwilling, almost afraid, to push the question further. She had already gone beyond anything she had been asked to do. Emtee Dempsey assumed she would come directly home after dropping Adam Fenwick off. But Kim had wanted to take the chance to find out if Dunning had been here that day.

"Is the women's locker room distinct from the men's?"

The question elicited ribald laughter, which was answer enough.

"The point of the question is to find out whether it is possible that a man went to Lydia's locker and took her clubs."

"No way," Fritz said.

"Benny is the only man who would go in there and he has a whistle he blows twice first. If no one objects, he goes in."

"What for?"

"Benny cleans clubs after they've been used. Players leave them at the shop, he cleans them up and puts them away in their lockers."

"I wonder why he didn't clean Lydia's?"

Fritz looked at her, then said slowly, "Because she didn't use her clubs to play golf with."

As soon as Kim emerged from the front door the car began to move out of the parking lot and came to where she stood. The driver came around the car but before opening the door he said to Kim, "You're supposed to call Sister Mary Teresa."

Kim turned to go back inside but the driver stopped her.

"Use the phone in the car."

He eased away from the front door and glided down the drive some twenty yards to park while Kim was dialing the number of the house on Walton Street.

"I am telephoning you from Mr. Rush's automobile," she said when Emtee Dempsey came on the line.

"Marvelous. Maybe we should get a phone for our car."

"Well, it's the size of a phonebooth."

"Where are you phoning from?"

"The Elm Stand Town and Country Club."

"Parked?"

174

"Yes."

"Good. Sister Kimberly, I called you for several reasons. First, Mr. Rush had to take a cab here to advise me on the charges that have been made against me and—"

"Charges! What charges?"

"And doubtless would like his car back."

"What charges are you talking of?"

"I am afraid Lydia inadvertently let it be known that she sought and found refuge in this house. Richard was infuriated for reasons I do not pretend to understand. In any case, Mr. Raymond Monday, the prosecutor, is here, along with Richard, putting an endless series of questions to me about the events of the last several days. Naturally, I telephoned Timothy Rush. I have also asked Katherine to come. Needless to say, I want you by my side."

"I'll come immediately."

"I knew you would. You have parted with Mr. Fenwick?"

"Yes."

A sigh came over the wire. "I know this is a nuisance, but do you suppose he would be willing to come back with you? Annoying as this legal harassment is, it may well prove providential. In any case, I think the time has come to liberate Lydia from her predicament by identifying the murderer. Mr. Fenwick, being one of the players in this drama, should be here."

"I'll do my best," Kim said, wondering how the elderly retired pro would react to the proposal that he repeat the round trip to Walton Street.

"Oh, and Sister. Do you think you could bring Benny along as well?"

"Benny!"

"I know." Another sigh. "A cast of thousands. But the

175

culmination requires that all the *dramatis personae* be on-stage."

"Sister, Benny is a very simple person."

"I understand that. Do you think you can persuade him to come here?"

"I'll do my best."

"I am sure that will more than suffice."

Which might have been the most fulsome praise Kim had ever received from Sister Mary Teresa. She told the driver to wait again in the parking lot. She was close to the pro shop and Benny, so she would start with him. The driver made a gesture with his gloved hand. He was at her disposal.

But as Kim went between the boxwood hedges beside the clubhouse to the golf shop, she wondered if it wouldn't have been wiser to have the car brought around. She could have enticed Benny inside by offering to show him all the gadgets. But she didn't want to go back now. Nor did she anticipate much trouble in getting Benny to come talk with Emtee Dempsey. But he proved remarkably reluctant.

"Talk about what?" he asked, his limpid eyes on hers.

Again Kim had the sense of a child looking out of a man's face.

"Lydia Hopkins."

The bony mass above his eyes descended in a frown. "You're always asking people about Mrs. Hopkins."

"I want to help her."

"Mr. Fenwick wanted to help her and they put her back in jail."

He kept backing away from her as they talked, moving among the various wares of the pro shop, as if all he wanted in life was the peace and quiet of the workroom in the back.

"I am going to ask Mr. Fenwick to come, too. Why don't you and I go ask him if he would?"

He stopped moving backward. "I'll go if Mr. Fenwick goes."

"Could we go get Mr. Fenwick in your cart, Benny? He will want to ride back to the car."

"Okay. I won't take my scooter."

"You can show me the way you went taking those things to Mr. Fenwick's garage."

He plodded toward the door as if he were going through hip-deep mud, but when Kim emerged he was already behind the wheel of a pale yellow golf cart. Kim got onto the seat beside him and he indicated the seat belt. She dutifully fastened it. The golf cart eased into motion and soon they were going at a surprising speed up the road flanked by beech and walnut trees. Benny hunched over the wheel and stared straight ahead, concentrating on directing the cart up the narrow road.

"Do you remember many years ago when the police were looking for Mrs. Hopkins's golf clubs, Benny?"

He looked briefly at her, then turned back to the road.

"They couldn't find them," Kim said, wondering why she didn't shut up. What, after all, did Benny understand?

He left the road, went through an open gate and onto the golf course aiming in a lazy diagonal at a rain shelter built behind two tees. It seemed to be their destination, but Kim didn't object. She had asked him to show her how he had taken the clubs to Fenwick's garage and that is no doubt what he was doing. At the shelter, Benny stopped the cart and turned the key. He turned to her, apparently ready to talk. One thing at a time.

"She left her clubs in the shop."

"Mrs. Hopkins?"

"Yes."

177

"To be cleaned?"

"They weren't dirty. She didn't use them much. But they were in the shop, next to my bench. When the police came, I went to get the clubs. They weren't there."

"Gone?"

He nodded.

"So you couldn't give them to the police?"

"I wouldn't do that. I wanted to hide them, so they couldn't hurt her."

"Did you tell anyone the clubs were gone?"

"I went to her locker. I can go in there, the police had to wait. Her clubs were there, in her locker."

"And you took them out?"

"I hid them. I hid them again in Mr. Fenwick's garage, when Mr. Byron told me to take the other stuff there."

"Why did you hide them?"

"I wish they were still where I put them. She's back in jail. Everyone talks about her." His lips folded in and he frowned under the bill of his cap.

"Mr. Fenwick was trying to help her when he gave them to the police."

"I know that."

"Did anyone ever talk to you, Benny?"

He looked at her in disbelief. "Naw. I'm retarded, you know."

"I know."

He seemed glad that was understood. "That doesn't matter to Mrs. Hopkins. To Mr. Fenwick neither. Other people . . ." He shook his head.

And what would Benny have told the police if they'd talked to him? He could not have stood up long to questioning and that incriminating golf club might have figured in Lydia's first trial. How ironic that Lydia's friends proved the greatest threat to her claim to be innocent. Her former claim. Only Sister Mary Teresa was unflagging in her belief in Lydia's innocence. What a champion the old nun was.

And now she stood in danger of legal retribution as well as the humiliation of having promised to do what she could not do. It wrung Kim's heart to hear Emtee Dempsey talk as if she were about to pull a rabbit out of a hat as she had so often in the past. Everything was against that now. Kim did not relish the thought of returning to Walton Street. Having so many others there would be a mixed blessing—it might cushion the blow, but it increased the number of witnesses to the revelation that Sister Mary Teresa was fallible after all.

But it was Lydia she should be thinking of. Emtee Dempsey could take care of herself, she always had.

Looking out over the fairway from Benny's cart, she asked herself if anything Benny had said could help Lydia. One of Lydia's clubs had been used to kill her husband and daughter and then it had been returned to her bag in the pro shop, brought from the house back to the Elm Stand. Lydia had come to the club, escaping a terrible quarrel with her husband, wanting to talk with Adam Fenwick. Apparently she also met William Dunning at the club. He sent her to a motel before the murders became known and then proceeded to the bar where he had very conspicuously and over much of the remainder of the afternoon consumed three very strong drinks.

How did the club get back into Lydia's bag? How did her bag get back into her locker?

Kim had no doubt how the prosecutor would answer the first question, but what about the second?

Benny hadn't put those clubs back in Lydia's locker. He had found them there and removed them. Who had put them there? Who else knew then what had happened in Elmhurst?

William Dunning.

An awful thought occurred. Had Dunning put Lydia's bag back in her locker? But that made no sense. Far from helping his client, her lawyer would have put the incriminating evidence just where the police must find it.

But why would he do a thing like that?

Someone had put the evidence in Lydia's locker and that someone must have been astounded when the locker was found to be empty.

Who?

"That's Mrs. Merrill's house," Benny said, pointing. "You can see her pool. She drowned there."

"I know."

"I hated her."

"Why?"

"She said bad things about Mrs. Hopkins."

"She was scared."

"She was bad."

The breeze coming over the mown grass of the fairway was hot but it was comfortable in the shade of the shelter. A threesome of golfers was moving away along the fairway, parallel to the sixteenth, but no one was approaching. Kim felt that she was inhabiting Benny's special universe now, one in which people were simply bad or good, the judgment based perhaps on how they treated him or those he liked.

Across the fairway, Adam Fenwick emerged from his house and stood on the patio above the pool, looking across at them. Kim waved and asked Benny to drive them toward Fenwick, who was giving her an answering wave.

A theatrical look of surprise seemed fixed on Adam Fenwick's face as they drew nearer in the cart. Benny brought it to a stop on the apron of Fenwick's pool.

"Sister, I saw you off in a limousine, and have you already fallen to this?"

"And glad to have the ride. I have an enormous favor to ask you. Sister Mary Teresa got in touch with me on the telephone in the car and asked if you could possibly return to Walton Street."

"Now?"

"It is a terrible imposition, but the police and prosecutor are there and they are threatening her because we gave Lydia refuge when they were looking for her."

"That's nonsense!"

"Apparently not to the police."

"Sister Kimberly, I owe that grand lady much. But what on earth can I do to help her?"

Kim hesitated, but had to say it. "She says she is going to solve Lydia's problem by identifying the murderer."

"She knows who did it?"

"That's what she says."

Adam Fenwick was nonplussed. "Do you think she does?"

"Yes." Once she said it, Kim felt lighter, but not with elation. It was like denying the Principle of Contradiction, bidding good-bye to reason, an exhilarating experience, but only momentarily.

"That's good enough for me."

Adam Fenwick got behind the wheel of the cart and Benny crouched in back, his expression one of excitement. This was turning into an adventure. Kim told Fenwick where the car was parked, and in a few minutes the three of them were in the backseat, Benny engrossed with the television. Adam Fenwick laid his hand on Kim's.

"How I hope she can do it, Sister. Imagine, if Lydia were free."

Kim nodded and looked away. Emtee Dempsey was about to take a great fall and many others would go down with her. Poor Adam Fenwick, dreaming of being reunited with the young woman he now believed was his daughter.

The great car took them swiftly through the western suburbs, into the Loop, where the driver turned north, and soon they were on Walton Street.

Kim had never felt sadder at coming home.

Ten

The house seemed to have been turned into a public arena.

Gleason and O'Connell stood glumly on the porch. Were they posted there as a precaution, lest Sister Mary Teresa make a bolt for freedom? Several squad cars were parked at the curb on either side of the street and uniformed officers lounged in the front seats of each.

"Come inside and have a beer," Kim said to Richard's assistants. (He had called them his "two right-hand men" once in Emtee Dempsey's presence and drawn a chuckling rebuke.)

They looked at her impassively, then Gleason shook his head. The door opened and Joyce looked out with a worried expression.

"We're all in the living room," she said, acknowledging Fenwick.

"This is Benny," Kim said.

Joyce stuck out her hand and Benny looked at it a moment before taking it. Fenwick had put a reassuring hand on his former employee's shoulder. He looked at Kim, who had been unable on the drive over to give him anything like an explanation of why Benny was with them.

"How many is 'all'?" he asked Joyce.

Kim said, "Why don't you take Benny into the kitchen, Joyce." She tried to convey in a look what she did not want to put into words. But Joyce got the picture. Big as Benny was, he was just a boy.

"I'm having ice cream," Joyce said to him. "Want some?"

"What kind?"

"What kind do you like?"

"You got any chocolate?"

"Let's find out."

And off they went. Adam Fenwick nodded in appreciation. "Benny is not at his best with a lot of people. Neither am I, for that matter."

All the more reason not to delay any longer.

"They'll be in the living room."

It was a larger crowd than even Kim was prepared for. And the reason for the special security was immediately obvious. In the center of one of the couches that flanked the fireplace sat Lydia Hopkins, serene, erect, in the room but not of it. Next to her was a woman who had to be a cop. When Adam Fenwick came through the door, Lydia's expression melted. Kim heard a little gasp from Fenwick.

"Thank heavens you're here," cried Emtee Dempsey, and the room fell silent. "Mr. Fenwick, I am extremely grateful to you for coming back here. I assure you that this annoyance will be brief."

Richard was looking everywhere but at Kim, as well he might. She did not give him credit for his sheepishness.

184

To add the indignity of a legal charge to the impending embarrassment of the old nun was unforgivable.

Monday, the prosecutor, said to a willowy woman in a baggy, oversize, extremely chic getup that the woman was another nun and the man Adam Fenwick. She wrote it down quickly in her steno pad.

"All right," the prosecutor said, addressing them all. "I know why I'm here. It beats me what most of you are doing here, but this is a private house and you've been invited and I can't do anything about that." He looked at his watch and his secretary followed suit. "All right. I agreed to postpone doing my job and I kept my promise. Moriarity."

Richard, trying to behave like a robot, pulled a paper from his pocket. "Sister Mary Teresa, this is a warrant for your arrest—"

That was as far as he got. Timothy Rush rose to his feet, talking as he did so; Katherine laughed derisively from the chair she sat in and then proceeded to say what she thought of such goings-on. William Dunning added to the chorus and soon the air was filled with questions, assertions, and accusations. Was this not a religious house? If so, what of the division of church and state? What evidence was there that Sister Mary Teresa had harbored a fugitive from justice and deliberately misled the police?

Monday looked startled by the intensity of the reaction and got his shoulder blades against the wall as if he feared this would come to violence. His secretary gave up trying to get it all down in shorthand. Sister Mary Teresa sat in her brocade chair like a female Buddha, eyes sparkling, but as dismayed as she was pleased. She showed her pudgy hand, imploring everyone to be quiet, but for once she was ignored in her own house. Meanwhile, calm as the eye of a storm, Lydia looked at Adam Fenwick and Adam

185

Fenwick looked at her, both oblivious to the surrounding commotion.

Kim took the opportunity to kneel next to Emtee Dempsey's chair and give her a swift but thorough résumé of everything she had learned at the club. Then she stood up and said in the loudest voice she could muster, "Will you all please be quiet and sit down!"

The silence was not instantaneous, but Kim had their attention.

"Sit down and be quiet, please. You are guests in this house. This house is a convent. Sister Mary Teresa is its Superior. If there is any further behavior of this kind, I will ask you all to leave."

Call it the power of the nun, call it the irresistible authority of an irate woman. Whatever the explanation, the room was now filled with a subdued and docile group. From where she stood beside the fireplace, Beverly John brought her hands together in silent applause. Kim turned to Emtee Dempsey.

"I believe you called everyone here for a particular purpose, Sister."

Emtee Dempsey's blue eyes twinkled with admiration, but then she nodded briskly and got down to business.

"The warrant Lieutenant Moriarity was about to read accuses me of providing sanctuary to a young woman wanted by the police, Mrs. Lydia Hopkins. My alleged guilt can thus be only a participation in her alleged guilt. Lydia has previously been tried and wrongly found guilty of two particularly horrendous murders. An acute jurist reviewed the trial and found it as wanting technically as it was substantively and let Lydia go. Nonetheless, Lydia is once again accused of those earlier murders and a third has been added to them. I propose to show that she did not commit any murders whatsoever and her innocence will entail my own and finally true justice can be done."

·

"You're going to prove Lydia Hopkins innocent?" Monday asked, as if he wanted this for the record.

"No, Mr. Monday. I am going to show that someone else is guilty. I need not tell you that our common presumption must be that Lydia Hopkins is innocent."

"But she admitted—"

"I object," cried William Dunning.

"That will do," Emtee Dempsey said sharply to the two lawyers. "This will take a good deal less time, if you let me proceed without undue interruption."

Kim became aware of the expression on Katherine Senski's face and it seemed the objective correlative of what she herself felt. Katherine was filled with admiration at her old friend's familiar confidence. The old nun was a stranger to doubt and it was tempting to believe that she would do now what she had done before. But, like Kim, Katherine apparently didn't believe this was possible. And that is why the crisp and masterly summary that followed was an agony to listen to. Sister Mary Teresa was fueling the engine of her own destruction.

"On the face of it, you may think there is new evidence, the mysteriously absent golf club, which tests have now proved to have been the—or at least, a—murder weapon. That Lydia Hopkins, on the occasion of the identification of that weapon, publicly claimed to have committed those crimes lends credence to the view that she did as she said. Of course, she did nothing of the kind. Consider a first and obvious fact. The club that was used as a weapon in Elmhurst had to find its way back to the country club."

"Where Lydia Hopkins immediately went after leaving the scene of the crime," Monday said.

"Correction. Lydia left her home in Elmhurst and drove to the Elm Stand Country Club to talk with Adam Fenwick and later meet with her lawyer, William Dunning."

"How do I stand corrected?"

"She left before the commission of the crimes."

"How can you say that?"

Emtee Dempsey smiled sweetly at the prosecutor. "Because Lydia has informed me of the fact. And now we have a corroborator. Mr. Fenwick, you remember that February day, do you not?"

All eyes turned to Adam Fenwick and he stroked his mustache nervously. But he soon recovered his aplomb and nodded.

"Lydia arrived at the club and the two of you sat at a table in the pro shop where, I gather, in season golfers sometimes have a soft drink between rounds."

"After nine holes, yes. It's quicker and less hectic than the bar."

"And profitable?"

He conceded this with a smile. "I made a dollar or two selling sodas. Byron retained the table but not the practice of selling soft drinks. Lydia and I often sat at that table talking."

"And did again that February day?"

"She was very upset."

Katherine stirred uneasily and Beverly John shifted her feet. They both seemed afraid that once again Adam Fenwick would say something detrimental to Lydia's case.

"I'm sure she was," Emtee Dempsey said. "Tell the others why."

Adam looked at Lydia as if for approval. "They had an awful fight. The worst ever. She said she just couldn't take it anymore and that she was going to go through with the divorce she had often threatened. I told her to call her lawyer right away."

"And she did?"

"Yes. William Dunning. He said he would come immediately."

Emtee Dempsey leaned to one side, to get a better look at Lydia. "Did you talk with William Dunning himself, Lydia?"

"To his secretary."

"Who said she would get the message to him as soon as he came in."

"Yes."

"Does that match your own memories, Mr. Dunning?" Emtee Dempsey asked.

"What I remember is that Lydia called me to the club so we could discuss her taking divorce action. I don't remember the details."

"Wouldn't you remember if you yourself took the call?"

"I sure would."

"Then you didn't."

"Sister, I almost never answer the telephone in my office. That's one reason I'd remember."

"But you don't recall how precisely the message got to you?"

"That's right, I don't. The main thing is that I got it and went to the club."

"At what time?"

Dunning looked thoughtfully at Emtee Dempsey. "Could you tell me what you're trying to find out?"

"These questions are expository rather than inquiring in nature. I am making the point that Lydia was at the club when those brutal killings took place in Elmhurst."

"I think we are going to have to prove that, Sister. Needless to say, I am eager to see if that can be done."

"Then remember when Lydia called your office. We know she placed that call from the pro shop. Do you remember what time that call was made, Mr. Fenwick?"

"It was just after two-thirty."

"You're sure?"

"I've thought of that day many, many times." He looked

at Lydia. "It broke my heart to hear the abuse she took from that man. But the reason I remember the time is that I took a pain pill for my arthritis and I have to note the time because I have to be careful of overdosing. It was just after two-thirty."

"Not nearly enough time to leave the Hopkins home after two and get to the club. Very well. And then she called William Dunning, who was not in his office. Now, Mr. Dunning, at what time did you arrive at the club?"

"I'm not sure. I don't have arthritis."

"Pray God you never do. But it was after two-thirty and before four o'clock."

"I suppose."

"No suppositions at all. These are facts. Lydia called you after two and Fritz the bartender began serving you strong drink from about four that afternoon."

"What are you getting at?"

"Well, Adam Fenwick has enabled us to see that Lydia was not at the house when the murders took place."

"Adam, don't," Lydia said, speaking softly but audibly, her tone one of affection laced with reproof. "Don't lie. You know it was much later that I got there."

Adam looked at her, astounded. "I know nothing of the kind."

Monday could not suppress a relieved smile. He had been following Emtee Dempsey's recital with some anxiety and he welcomed this apparent puncturing of the balloon. But the old nun looked even more pleased than the prosecutor.

"Let us establish the motivation for Lydia's remark, Adam. Were you surprised when Lydia came to the club that day?"

"No. She called first. In fact, I heard from her several times that day. A running account of the fight with Jeff. It had gone on and on and every once in a while she would shut herself up in her bedroom and call me."

"What were you doing when Lydia took your advice and came to the club?"

"I wasn't back yet."

"Back from where?"

"I had lunch at home because I like a little nap afterward."

"Does that set your mind at ease, Lydia?" the old nun asked. "You do not have to claim to have done what you did not do in order to protect someone else."

"Do you mean me! Lydia . . ." Adam Fenwick crossed the room to the couch. The female cop stood and the elderly man sat beside Lydia. "My God, did you think that I did those awful things?"

Lydia took his hand in hers and seemed to share his incredulity.

"Now then," the old nun said, calling them to order. "Lydia, when did you put your golf clubs back in your locker?"

"I didn't tell you that," Lydia said.

"Then tell me now. Did you put your golf bag back in your locker?"

"Yes."

"Where was the bag?"

"In the golf shop, the room in back. Bill Dunning and I went there to talk in privacy. That's when he told me what had happened at the house. The whole day had been a series of shocks. Perhaps that is what enabled me not to collapse under that final one. I looked across the room and saw my golf bag. I remembered I had left it there in the fall and was surprised it was still there."

"And you noticed something else."

"How do you know that?"

"You saw that one of the clubs was dirty and stained, and then you saw that it was blood. Isn't that how it was?"

"Yes."

"And you rushed precipitously to the conclusion that Adam Fenwick, who all that day had been hearing stories of the legendary quarrel going on in your home, had taken that club, gone to the house and killed your husband."

Lydia began to nod halfway through Emtee Dempsey's statement, but she had turned to Adam Fenwick as if to ask his forgiveness.

"Good Lord, Laura was killed too. Surely you didn't think . . ."

But Emtee Dempsey still had the floor. "There then are two points. First, Lydia did not kill her husband and daughter. Second, she claimed she had because she suspected Adam Fenwick was their killer. Who then put the bloody club in that golf bag? Obviously, the killer. And who was that? Let us proceed systematically. Lydia, your lawyer suggested that you go to a hotel, is that right?"

"A motel."

"And you did?"

"Yes."

Monday droned, "All that is in the transcript of the trial."

"Indeed," the old nun said. "And we are learning how much is not in that transcript. The time Lydia arrived at the motel is there, however. Do you recall when it was, Mr. Monday?"

"I think you want to tell me."

"It was four-fifty-five. The motel is not ten minutes from the club. So what do we have? Mr. Dunning is in the bar drinking scotch from approximately four o'clock. Sometime prior to that he has advised his client to get a good night's rest in a motel."

192

Monday stifled a derisive laugh. "Maybe we should serve that warrant on you, Dunning."

"During this interval, someone took Lydia's golf bag from the pro shop and put it into her locker. Why? So that when it was found there, the finger of suspicion would point to her. Who made that transfer? When Lydia saw the bloody club in the workroom of the pro shop, she was not alone. William Dunning was with her."

"My God, I hope you're not suggesting that I put it there," Dunning said in a shocked tone.

"Did you?"

"No!"

"I did." Lydia said. "I put the clubs in my locker."

"Of course," the old nun said. "And then someone took them out again."

"Was that you, Dunning?" Richard asked.

"I'll forget you said that, Moriarity," Dunning said.

"You didn't answer the question," Monday pointed out.

"Ask him why he tried to get one of my employees to steal a report out of my office." Beverly John stepped in front of the fireplace when she said this and looked sharply at Dunning.

"Oh for God's sake," Dunning said in disgust.

"If you wanted it you could have come to me."

"What report are we talking about?" Monday asked Beverly John. "Some investigation you did?"

"For Mrs. Hopkins. If she had asked for it, I would have turned it over. But he wanted it stolen and paid good money for it."

Dunning was shaking his head in disgust. "Yes, and I could have subpoenaed it and then the prosecutor would have gotten a look at it too."

This set off a spate of legalistic moralizing from Monday. Emtee Dempsey turned to Kim and beckoned her close.

"Did you bring Benny with you?"

"He's in the kitchen with Joyce."

"Take him to my study, would you please?"

"Your study?"

"I think it is time we offered these people refreshments. That is going to keep Joyce busy."

Sister Mary Teresa announced a recess and enlisted Katherine to help Joyce take orders from the assembly. Kim went into the kitchen, where Joyce and Benny sat at opposite sides of the kitchen table leafing through issues of *Sports Illustrated*.

"How's it going?"

"Joyce, she's incredible."

"I already knew that. Is she in trouble?"

"No! I think she's done it. She wants you. Time for drinks."

"That usually means things are going well."

Benny followed their conversation, a little boy mystified by adults. Kim said, "Benny, I want to show you another room. Did you have ice cream?"

"Chocolate."

"Good." But Kim did not have Joyce's knack. She was about to tell Benny she would show him walls and walls of books, but she realized that was unlikely to impress or interest him. But she did not have to offer him an explanation. He was content in this house and would do as he was told. "Come on."

He came down the hall after her. She went into the study first and he followed her. He looked around the room with disinterest until he saw the typewriter on which Kim did Emtee Dempsey's business correspondence.

"Would you like to type?"

He did. She put a piece of paper in and got him seated

before the machine. She turned the switch and he began to move the carriage back and forth like a machine gun, grinning like the boy he essentially was. Ten minutes later, Emtee Dempsey came in, followed by Monday, Timothy Rush, and Dunning. The men were carrying glasses. And then Lydia came in. The old nun stood beside Benny and put her hand on his shoulder, reminding Kim of the way Adam Fenwick had reassured Benny when they arrived at the house.

"You are as good a typist as Sister Kimberly," she told him.

Benny did a double take when he looked up and saw this little old woman with the huge headdress standing beside him. Children are either frightened by or fascinated with nuns in habits. Benny was fascinated.

"Isn't it a strange hat that I wear, Benny?"

He grinned. And then he noticed Lydia and immediately got to his feet and went to her. Hands at his sides, he stood in front of her, waiting. Lydia gave him a sweet, sad smile and took him in her arms.

"How are you, Benny?"

"They told me you got out."

"I should have come to see you."

Sister Mary Teresa pointed out that the room was too small for all of them to sit but that, with their permission, she was going to occupy her chair behind the desk. Who had likened talking with the old nun to a visit to the principal's office? The four men—Dunning, Rush, Monday, and Benny—formed a semicircle before the desk. Lydia and Kim stayed in the background. The old nun spoke less dramatically now, her tone suggesting they were all on the same side now.

"I said I would identify the one you seek. He is here in this room. The first question is, who took Lydia Hopkins's golf bag from her locker?"

195

Kim looked at Lydia. Suddenly she understood what had happened. My God. She made room for herself between Benny and Mr. Rush.

"Benny," she said, "tell Sister Mary Teresa what you told me."

"Benny!" Dunning backed off to stare at the pro shop employee.

"Benny," repeated the old nun. "Yes, Benny. There was no one else after I eliminated you, Mr. Dunning. There was some unlikelihood that even in February you could have gotten into and out of the women's locker room without being noticed, whereas for Benny that posed no problem."

Benny had picked up a glass paperweight from the desk and was watching snow fall on a fat little Santa inside the glass globe.

"Are you saying he killed Jeffrey and Laura?"

"Why don't you ask him, Mr. Monday?"

"No, Sister," Lydia said. "Please. I'll ask him."

The men stepped back and Lydia took one of the chairs across from Emtee Dempsey and had Benny sit beside her. He kept the glass paperweight.

Looking at him, Lydia began to talk musingly, as if to herself. "He was always there when I would talk to Adam. He must have heard me talk about Jeff. He came once a week to do our lawn and more than once he saw Jeff when he was acting crazy. I remember that once he even said he would do something to anyone who hurt me. I never thought of that until a few minutes ago. Benny?"

He looked up.

"Benny, you took my clubs from the locker, didn't you?"

"I hid them."

"Why?"

"I heard the police wanted them. They were supposed

196

to be in the shop, only they were gone. So I checked your locker and they were there. I hid them."

"Do you remember anything else that day?"

"What?"

Lydia was breathing shallowly now and her eyes were alight with a mixture of emotions. She took Benny's hand. He looked directly at her.

"What happened at the house, Benny?"

"I'm sorry."

"Tell me what happened."

"Him, that was okay. He said bad things about you. He got out that gun. I took it away from him but I couldn't hit him with it. I'm no good at that. I needed the club first."

Lydia had drawn her upper lip between her teeth and was biting down on it.

"I got really mad. It was bad."

Tears spilled from Lydia's eyes as she nodded.

"I didn't mean to hurt the little girl. But she *saw* me. And she began to scream. I'm real sorry about her."

The study was so quiet they could hear the murmur of voices from the living room. Emtee Dempsey looked at Monday. "I think that is enough, don't you? You will want to ask Benny about Dolores Merrill."

"She said very bad things about you," Benny said, still looking at Lydia. "Mrs. Hopkins, please don't cry. I don't like it when you cry. I thought you would never cry again."

Lydia burst into helpless sobbing then and Benny, his face twisted in uncomprehending agony, put the paperweight on the desk and patted her hand with his pawlike one.

Richard came in and then Gleason and O'Connell and Benny was taken away. The murderer had been found, but there would be no trial.

"I am so sorry, Lydia," Emtee Dempsey said. "I knew

from the beginning that however the matter would be explained there was more pain in store for you. Not that we can really blame Benny. The poor man thought he was doing good."

"How did you know it was him?"

"From what Sister Kimberly told me. Unlike you, I did not imagine Adam Fenwick could have done the deed. And William Dunning? Nonsense. He was risking his career to save you. There was no one left but Benny."

Richard said, "How could he get to the house and back without being seen? He must have been a mess afterward."

"The same way he went to do the Hopkinses' lawn. On his motor scooter. He took the club he was working on with him. Lydia's club."

"What did he do with his bloody clothes?"

"Where have Lydia's golf clubs been all these years?"

There was silence in the study. Was everyone thinking of Benny on his motor scooter, off on his grim errand to stop Jeff Hopkins from making Lydia cry? The madness of the murder scene matched the mind of Benny. What had Jeff said to enrage him so? And poor little Laura . . .

When Lydia was composed, they went back to the living room where Emtee Dempsey gave Katherine and Beverly John a swift version of what had happened.

"Sister Mary Teresa, you have done it again," Katherine cried. "I don't mind telling you I was certain that this time you would regret saying what you did."

"Saying what I did?"

"Offering to identify the real murderer."

"But why should this time be different? The credit goes to Sister Kimberly. It is she who finds these things out, not I."

"Of course, you have in a sense failed, Sister," Katherine said.

"In what sense?" Emtee Dempsey said, looking sharply at her old friend.

"You have provided the one who killed Jeffrey and Laura as well as Dolores Merrill. But what of Mildred Pilsudski?"

"What of her?"

Kim said, "The other night you gave as the basis for your conviction that Lydia was innocent that she could not have killed Mildred Pilsudski."

"Mildred Pilsudski killed herself."

"That's being contested!" Katherine objected.

"Sister," Kim said. "You quite definitely said that whoever killed the other three also killed Mildred Pilsudski."

"That was my working hypothesis for a time, true. But I checked with Richard just this afternoon. It seems that no one killed Mildred Pilsudski. The coroner now agrees with the family that it was an accident. She started the motor and could not get the garage door to respond to a remote control device. Her persistent trying proved her undoing. Now, *if* she had been murdered, you could reasonably hold me to my earlier statement."

"Sister Mary Teresa, you are incorrigible!" Katherine cried.

"It would grieve me to think that is true," the old nun said, but she was clearly pleased as she could be.

Meanwhile Lydia and Adam Fenwick were talking with Beverly John. That conversation and some subsequent checking proved what Lydia had suspected from Beverly John's report. Her mother had been Adam Fenwick's Sarah. What had the old pro called a nun's life? A life lived behind a veil of ignorance. Well, that is how his life had been lived, but now the veil was lifted for father and daughter, and Lydia, having cruelly lost her daughter and husband, was restored to the father she had never known.

199

Sister Mary Teresa advised her to put off thoughts of a religious life for now.

"Your primary duty is to your father. Each of you has need of the other now."

Monday sought and received maximum coverage in the media when he explained why Lydia Hopkins would not be brought to trial. Benny was a three-day wonder in the media—his bloodstained clothes were found in a sand trap where he said he had buried them—but when the story died he was confined to a psychiatric hospital. It was unlikely that he would ever be released. Lydia, mindful of her own time in prison, visited Benny regularly. Her request that she might take Benny for a visit to the house on the edge of the sixteenth fairway she shared with her father was regularly turned down.

And in the little chapel of the house on Walton Street, for some months after these events, Jeffrey and Laura Hopkins, Dolores Merrill, and Mildred Pilsudski received special mention in the prayers for the departed with which the three members of the Order of Martha and Mary ended each day.